Death by
the Book

Death by the Book

LENNY BARTULIN

MINOTAUR BOOKS

A THOMAS DUNNE BOOK
NEW YORK

A THOMAS DUNNE BOOK FOR MINOTAUR BOOKS.
An imprint of St. Martin's Publishing Group.

DEATH BY THE BOOK. Copyright © 2008 by Lenny Bartulin. All rights reserved. Printed in the United States of America. For information, address St. Martin's Press, 175 Fifth Avenue, New York, N.Y. 10010.

www.thomasdunnebooks.com
www.minotaurbooks.com

Library of Congress Cataloging-in-Publication Data

Bartulin, Lenny.
    Death by the book / Lenny Bartulin. — 1st U.S. ed.
        p.   cm. — ("A Thomas Dunne book.")
    ISBN 978-0-312-55972-4
1. Booksellers and bookselling—Fiction.   I. Title.
    PR96619.4.B38D43   2010
    823'.92—dc22

                                                                      2009039811

First published as *A Deadly Business* in Australia by Scribe Publications

First U.S. Edition: January 2010

10   9   8   7   6   5   4   3   2   1

To Robert Gray

IT WAS PERFECTLY CLEAR TO HIM NOW, dangling in the wet tussock cleavage of a broad hill that slid towards the headland cliffs. Nothing like fresh air and imminent death to clarify things. Jack could see exactly when his life had begun to go downhill: it was that Wednesday afternoon a couple of weeks ago when he stepped off the bus in Double Bay. He had gone two stops past where he should have. A man susceptible to omens might have understood it as a warning. But Jack Susko thought it was his lucky day. Not having seen one for some time, it was an easy mistake to make.

The narrow ravine cut through the headland like an axe mark, straight down to the foot of the cliffs. A hundred metres below, Jack could hear waves smash into crags of rock and hiss over a coarse gravel beach. When he had slipped, the handcuffs had somehow tangled with a discarded piece of harness strap and the branches of a small tree. The strap must have come from one of the weekend hang-gliders; Jack had seen them run down the smooth hill before, watched them lift off with a slight dip and then curve out over the water like giant, lazy birds. It was a nice view up there, off the cliffs: a perfect spot for a romantic picnic. Somewhere to crack the champagne and propose marriage. All you needed was the right girl.

Jack craned his head up. 'Hey, listen,' he called out. 'What do you say we get married? Right now? We could kidnap a priest and bring him back.'

She was standing three or four metres above him, looking down. Holding a gun. She held it casually by her side like a mobile phone. The morning sky was dark with rain clouds but clearing. Jack could just make out her face: pale and thin like watered-down milk. As though another burst of rain might wash her away.

Her gun hand came up slowly, empty eye down the barrel-sight. Her blank gaze fixed on something beyond him, way down in the blackness below. She was giving Jack *the look*, the one Ziggy Brandt had warned him about a long time ago.

They were in the big black Mercedes with the customised number plates: EASY. Jack at the wheel, suit and tie, but a little dark under the eyes. It was after three in the morning. Ziggy was stretched out in the back, legs spread wide. 'You got to watch it, Jack, you got to watch that look,' he said, voice on the edge of slurring after a few too many at his club in the Cross. 'I call it the seven veils look. They're looking at you, but nobody's home. You know what I mean?'

Jack nodded into the rear-view mirror, half-listening. Ziggy brushed invisible crumbs from his Armani duds. 'Be ready for that look, Jack. Nine times out of ten it's followed by a fucking bullet.' He laughed, then coughed. 'The other time it's either a knife or they push your eyeballs into your head with a hammer.'

The handcuffs were holding but Jack was reluctant to try pulling himself up. He moved a leg, feeling for a foothold. As he did, the gun went off. The bullet thudded into the ground near his shoulder. Grass and dirt stung his face. *Fuck*.

He should have minded his own business. Curiosity got the cat's head blown off.

'Honeymoon in Tahiti,' he shouted, desperation rising in his voice. 'Massages and cocktails by the pool. Nothing but the best, baby!' Jack was not into things tropical, but then marriage was all about compromise. 'If you could just throw me a rope ...'

The gun remained pointed at him.

Jack tried to squirm up the rain-drenched slope. Like a worm on the end of a hook. A surge of adrenaline helped move him about a foot. Not enough. And where the hell was he going anyway?

Another bullet hollowed out the dark and scorched the air not too far from his left ear, thumping into the soggy ground. Was she a terrible shot or just a sadistic bitch?

Jack closed his eyes, pressed himself against Mother Earth. Almost let slip a prayer, but it was too late to pay insurance now. 'How about a last cigarette?'

There was no reply. Waves broke below. Jack breathed in the cold salty air: but all he could taste was gunshot smoke and fear.

The strap slipped out. Then held. His body stiffened, turned to lead. Light rain began to fall again. Terror beat his heart. *Jesus. I'm gonna die.*

Who the hell was going to look after his cat?

~1~

THE SKY WAS TWO O'CLOCK BLUE, cloudless on a Wednesday afternoon. The weather had forgotten it was winter: the air was almost sweet and the breeze had manners. Jack Susko lit a cigarette and began walking down the hill. He could not remember the last time he was in Double Bay. Nobody he knew earned the sort of money needed to live here. It was the kind of place where old women noticed your shoes, where lawns were green year-round, and the streets were clean and wide and lined with big old trees. A place where money had always done the talking and everything else the listening—even the pollution had been slipped a roll and asked to go west. Parks and playgrounds and plenty in the bank: the kind of place to consider having kids.

Jack put his sunglasses on. Having a child was not a priority, though if you asked him what was he might take a while to answer. For the moment, it was a package he was delivering to 32 Cumberland Gardens. The streets were so nice around here, they were gardens.

Over the rooftops on his right, Jack caught glimpses of water in the bay. On his left, houses and apartment blocks stepped up the slope of Bellevue Hill, straining against each other for a better view, their windows whitewashed by the sun. Jack had a vision of himself in one of those double-glazed sunrooms: cognac in hand, looking out at the city's skyline, the phone warm on his ear as he gave calm instruction to a banker on the Bahnhof Strasse in Zurich. It was the kind of job he could settle for, part-time even. Pity they never came up in the employment pages.

No, Jack Susko would not be retiring at the age of thirty-four. His view would remain the dusty shelves and battered paperbacks of the last year or so. Instead of up, he would climb down the steps into his basement shop in York Street in the city, where he spent the day making sure delinquent kids did not lift the stock. At least he was his own boss. Though sometimes it would have been nice to boss somebody around.

The guy's name was Hammond Kasprowicz. He had called Jack two days ago, asking for copies of four books: *The Machine*, *Entropy House*, *The Cull* and *Simply Even*. Every copy you have, he said. And it's poetry, he added, as if Jack might not know what that was. Did Susko Books have a poetry section? His voice was cantankerous. At one point he coughed violently down the line for about a minute and Jack had to hold the phone away from his ear. When he stopped,

Kasprowicz wheezed and his voice was tight. He would pay fifty dollars for every copy and an extra fifty if they were personally delivered. He gave his address, stated a time and day, and hung up.

Afterwards, Jack wondered why Kasprowicz was willing to pay so much for very little. But he did not think about it for too long. He remembered a piece of advice he had been given many years ago: *when someone wants to give you money, the least you can do is dress nice and take it.* Jack could do that.

Unlike a lot of second-hand bookshops, Susko Books was an alphabetised affair. There were two copies of *The Cull* in the poetry section. After checking through a few boxes of the latest, unsorted stock, Jack made some calls. He managed to locate one more copy of *The Cull* and two copies of *Entropy House*. But it was late and most places around town were already closed. The next day he went to King Street in Newtown and scoured second-hand bookshops for an hour or two. That was all he could handle amid the mess and choked shelves and the floor littered with old orange Penguins, fallen like ticket stubs at the races. It was nauseating, like walking around in somebody else's headache. No copies of *Simply Even* that he could see, just one of *The Machine*, missing a few pages, but that was not his problem. Three hundred dollars plus another fifty dollars delivery. It did not happen every day. It had never happened before.

The poet was Edward Kass: the serious kind, treated to a capital P. Numerous awards, commendations, even a mention in the Queen's birthday honours list for 1981. The biographical details went on to say that his critically acclaimed work was: *innovative, dark, enigmatic and entertainingly idiosyncratic.* Jack had heard of him but not had the pleasure. He read a few poems on the bus and decided the style was overwrought; Edward Kass would probably have seen death in a bowl of cornflakes. Jack still could not help wondering why Kasprowicz was willing to pay so much for them. The editions themselves were nothing special—the usual pretentious covers and cheap paper, a few big publishers, a few small, a couple of overseas imprints. Nobody famous had signed or dedicated them to anyone. Fifty bucks? To Jack they were just another pile of forgotten books that nobody had the heart to send to the crematorium. He called them *in-between* books, the kind the second-hand dealer liked least: not classics and not recent releases. Sometimes the second-hand bookshop was like an old people's home.

Kasprowicz had said 2.30 p.m. Jack was going to be right on time. He turned into another street and admired the houses, the cars and the front gardens. As he picked his favourites, a couple of joggers thumped towards him: a bald middle-aged man wearing all the gear and breathing like a broken hand-pump, and a fat girl in her late twenties who would have looked uncomfortable walking. Approaching, they straightened up for Jack's benefit. Twenty metres down the road they slumped forward again, as though they were running through mud. So money could not buy everything after all.

From the street, 32 Cumberland Gardens was not much to look at, unless you had a thing for high sandstone walls and even higher pine trees. Jack stood and admired the barrier: thirty metres of it, simple and impenetrable like a cliff. You would not want to lock yourself out. The sandstone sat heavy and contented and did not reveal anything, except that here were people who liked privacy and could afford it. He pressed the buzzer on an intercom set between a door and a solid timber gate. After a while, a voice finally crackled back at him.

'Yes?'

'My name's Susko. I've got a delivery for a Mr Kasprowicz.'

There was no reply, just the click of a button being released. Then the door buzzed and Jack pushed it. As he walked through, he slipped the package under his arm and pulled at the cuffs of his cream shirt. He adjusted his chocolate-brown mohair scarf and re-buttoned his tan jacket. Ran a hand through his dark hair. He was looking good. Just then the gate behind him began to open. It shuddered as it slid along the length of the sandstone wall. Jack watched a metallic blue Audi A6 drive through. The windows were tinted blue-black and reflected his face. More privacy. He followed the car into the Kasprowicz property.

Surprisingly, the front yard was shabby and in need of a trim. Maybe the gardener was on holidays. Tufts of green weeds grew between the hexagonal blocks of the driveway. *Casa Kasprowicz* was a large Federation-style homestead with lichen-stained redbrick walls and sandstone corners. Big and sprawling but not as grand as Jack had expected. A verandah stretched across the front and continued around both sides. Dormer windows protruded from the tiled roof. Off the right-hand side there was a low, flat-roofed garage extension, to which the carport was attached. From there Jack heard the Audi's door slam. He waited for somebody to appear.

Four sandstone steps led up to the verandah. The front door was painted dark green, with a leadlight window above it: three small ovals contained within a larger half-circle. *Cumberland House* was written across the stained glass in old-fashioned gold lettering. Fancy stuff. Jack imagined what *Susko House* might look like up there.

'Can I help you?'

A woman approached him. There was a subtle swing to her hips. She wore sunglasses, a short, fitted, beige leather jacket, and a baby blue cashmere scarf draped over a matching silk camisole. Downstairs, dark brown tailored pants with a pale blue pinstripe, and cream suede mules. Easy style, all class. Long chestnut hair with plenty of volume. She got closer and Jack saw that she was tall, five foot seven or eight at least, and on the curvy side of womanhood. Enough to make a poor boy blush.

'I'm here to see a Mr Kasprowicz,' said Jack. 'The name's Susko.'

She removed her sunglasses and looked him over. 'Nice scarf.' With her little finger she pulled a stray hair out of the corner of her mouth. Then she flicked her hair back and it fell all over the place, perfectly. Jack guessed forty: a fit, sophisticated, no expenses spared kind of forty. He took his sunglasses off for a better view.

'Mr Kasprowicz, eh?' she said. 'Lucky you.' She looked Jack over some more but did not say if she liked anything else. Seemed as if the scarf was it.

He followed her up onto the verandah and through the front door. They entered a long, wide hallway, lit by skylights. There was a large antique sideboard near the entrance, with a carved wooden headboard and rectangular mirror inset. The walls were maroon and hung with paintings and some black-and-white photographs. A long Turkish runner covered the floor: the polished timber boards underneath creaked with age and history and money.

The woman stopped to flip through a small stack of mail. Jack put his hands in his pockets.

'Nice place,' he said.

'Do you think?' Her voice was uninterested. She tossed the mail and some car keys onto the sideboard. 'I'll get my father for you. You can wait in there.' She pointed ahead and then disappeared through a door on her left.

Jack walked to the end of the hallway and took two steps down. He entered a square lounge room with a high ceiling and moulded cornices. It was dark and on the stuffy side: somebody needed to open a window. There were three Chesterfields facing each other in the centre of the room, separated by two red leather armchairs, some rugs, tables and lamps. An upright piano in the far corner. On the walls, a couple of round mirrors and more paintings: portraits mainly, also three large nineteenth-century landscapes in gilt frames. Jack gave the nearer one some attention. It was unattractive, no doubt worth a packet: soggy green English hills, a soggy blue sky, a couple of soggy oak trees, a soggy grey Georgian-style country house, and a soggy red fox getting the hell out of there.

'I said two o'clock, Mr Susko.'

Jack turned around and watched Kasprowicz walk over to the couches. He was tall and broad, but age had dropped most of his bulk to his gut and thighs: all bottom-end now, like an old beanbag. He was dressed in brown corduroy pants and a black cardigan, buttoned up to the collar of a white shirt. Thick grey hair with streaks of nicotine-yellow, combed back over a square head. Close-set eyes hidden behind eyebrows you could lose a pencil in. Pale skin and a nose that looked like it had a walnut buried in the end of it. Not an attractive man. He lowered himself into one of the armchairs and exhaled loudly. The leather creaked around him like an old boat ready to sink.

'It's now two-thirty. I don't like it when I'm kept waiting.'

'Maybe I should leave?' In Jack's experience, the customer was always wrong.

Kasprowicz cough-laughed. He put his fist to his mouth and leaned forward. A little time passed before he resumed talking.

'Very quick,' he said. 'I presume you've got my books?'

Jack held up the package and Kasprowicz motioned for it. Jack passed it to him and sat down in one of the Chesterfields opposite.

Kasprowicz began tearing the brown paper wrapping. His face brightened. 'Ah, *The Cull*,' he said. 'And no fewer than three copies!' He flicked through the pages with his soft, wrinkled fingers. The nails were long and yellow and Jack did not like looking at them. 'What else have we got here, eh?'

Just then his daughter appeared in a doorway behind him. 'Where's Louisa?' she asked. A cigarette burnt in her right hand. Her tone held the fresh menace of a first-round jab.

Kasprowicz stiffened. 'Her father came for her.'

'Fuck,' she whispered, and left.

The old man looked at Jack. 'Have you met my daughter,

Annabelle? Wonderful girl.' He went back to the books on his lap. 'You've done well, Mr Susko. Three hundred dollars.'

'Plus delivery.'

The old man screwed up his face, like he had stepped on a snail. His eyes narrowed and pushed out his awful eyebrows. 'Would you be interested in more work?'

'Sure. Depends what it is.'

'I wouldn't offer you anything too complicated. I'd just like you to find as many Edward Kass books for me as you possibly can.' He clasped his ugly fingers over the books in his lap.

'How many are there?'

'Only the four titles I've requested. He was not prolific.'

'No, I mean how many are there in the world?'

'Not as many as you might think. You should know editions of poetry are never very large. But it would add up for you. I'm sure you need the money.'

Jack smiled and removed his scarf. He leaned forward and held it between his legs. 'The world's a big place, Mr Kasprowicz. Who knows where they've all ended up.' But Jack was doing the sums in his head.

'I doubt the world has seen them.' Kasprowicz sat up and put the books and wrapping paper on a glass table beside him. 'I've got all the publishing details, how many books were printed, where, when, all that. From memory, it's only about four thousand copies.'

'And you want all of them?' asked Jack, raising an eyebrow. He was going to ask if the old man expected him to steal copies from the library.

Kasprowicz frowned. 'Isn't fifty dollars a copy worth it,

Mr Susko? I can always find someone else, if you prefer.'

'No, it's worth it.'

'Good. Cash okay?' The old man gave a wry grin.

'Eight days a week.'

Kasprowicz grabbed the arms of the chair and hauled himself up. A phone began to ring on a small desk. 'Let's do an advance,' he said over the ringing. 'To inspire *application*. I already owe you three-fifty so ... let's say a nice clean thousand to start.' He walked over to the phone. 'Cash.' Hammond Kasprowicz smiled and put the receiver to his ear. 'Hello?'

A thousand bucks. Not bad for a Wednesday afternoon. Jack was starting to like the old guy.

Kasprowicz raised his voice into the telephone. 'Tony, we can't have this. No. No ... Oh, come on ... That's not a reason ... I'm putting the phone down, Tony ... Listen to me, Tony, I'm going to put the phone down ...'

Annabelle walked in. She stood in a thin shaft of light from one of the windows. Jack could see dust somersault through the air around her, full of glee.

'Would you like a drink, Mr Susko? My father has worked hard over the years to forget his manners.'

Kasprowicz slammed the receiver down, making Jack jump. The old man ignored his daughter as he walked past and out of the room. He paid even less attention to Jack.

Annabelle glared at her father. Jack heard a few knives whisper death through the air. Then she turned and smiled.

'Scotch? Gin? I think I might have a G & T.'

'Scotch, thanks. Neat.'

Annabelle made her way to a small metal-and-glass drinks stand and began pouring the drinks.

Jack got up and walked to the piano. 'Do you play?' he asked.

'God, no. It's just for show. Do you?'

Jack tinkled the keys. 'I fantasise.' He played a couple of the opening chords to Duke Ellington's 'Take the A Train'. On top of the piano he noticed two silver-framed photographs. One was of a cat, a copper-coloured Abyssinian with a white chin; the other, a grainy black-and-white of a sour-looking woman in her fifties. She wore a pearl necklace with a diamond pendant and matching earrings. The photographer had set her up in a movie-star pose. But Ava Gardner she was not: the face Jack looked at in the photograph knew it, too.

'Nice cat.'

'My mother's favourite. Jordan. She paid for a funeral when it died.' Kasprowicz's daughter brought Jack's drink over and passed it to him. 'I'm Annabelle,' she said.

'Your father told me.'

'Did he say what a pain in his arse I was?'

Jack grinned. 'No, he didn't mention it.'

She shrugged and sat down on one of the couches, crossing her long legs and slipping a hand between her thighs. 'That's my mother in the other photo. Her dying wish was that the cat's collar be buried with her.'

Jack picked up the photograph for a closer look. There was a resemblance between mother and daughter, but not much. The eyes that stared back at him were like ball-bearings. The lips were thin and the chin a little pointed. He had seen this type of woman before. He knew the corners of her mouth stayed turned down even when she smiled. The victim. Jack put the photograph back.

'Her greatest disappointment in life was that nobody was as interested in her as she was.'

'Aren't we all like that?'

'She was an expert. The best there ever was.' Annabelle sipped her drink. 'Do you smoke? I've just run out of cigarettes.'

Jack pulled out his pack and offered her one.

'Oh. These are strong, aren't they?'

'Just have half.'

He leaned over and lit the cigarette for her. Annabelle blew smoke and said: 'All this is my mother's, everything you see, the house, too. She was English, if you hadn't guessed.'

Jack sat down opposite Annabelle and snapped the lighter to his own cigarette. He noticed there were no rings on her long fingers, just a fine gold bracelet that slid down her wrist and hung on the cuff of her leather jacket as she held her cigarette in the air above her shoulder. There was a small, four-leafed clover attached to it.

'So what do you do, Mr Susko? What has my father got you in for?'

'Call me Jack. I'm a second-hand bookseller.'

Annabelle looked surprised. Then disappointed. 'Really. You must read a lot.'

'When it's slow.'

'And is it slow often?'

'Only Mondays to Fridays. And Saturdays.'

She tapped her cigarette into an ashtray on the table beside her. 'Oh, well.' She noticed the package of books her father had placed there. Her eyes narrowed as she read the title of the topmost book.

'So a bit of work on the side with my father?' she said, her voice rising in pitch. 'To make ends meet?'

'My ends never meet,' said Jack. 'They dislike each other too much.'

She managed to smile for two seconds. It exposed a slight dimple in her right cheek. She uncrossed and then crossed her legs again. She pushed herself back into the chair. The leather couch groaned beneath her like a dirty old man.

'What rare edition is he after this time?'

'Mr Susko doesn't deal with that kind of thing,' said Kasprowicz from the doorway. He walked back into the room like a bear. 'I doubt his business would have seen too much of any great value.'

Jack let it slide. There was a grand coming his way.

Annabelle got up and placed her drink on the coffee table. 'I'll leave you to your business.' Even through the tobacco smoke her perfume wafted over Jack. It smelt like five hundred dollars.

'Nice to meet you,' he said, as she left.

'Yes,' she replied, without looking at him.

Kasprowicz walked around and stood behind Jack. 'Here you are, Mr Susko.'

Jack extinguished his cigarette in the cut-glass ashtray before him and stood up.

Kasprowicz handed him a small white envelope. 'Maybe you could let me know in a week or two how it's all going.'

'Of course.'

'Goodbye.'

There was no handshaking. Kasprowicz walked off and left Jack to find his own way out.

He lingered a few seconds, looking about him. The house was silent: it felt suddenly empty and solemn, like a weekday church. Jack's gaze caught the photograph of Mrs Hammond Kasprowicz, on top of the piano. He stared at it a moment. For some reason, he thought that she would not have liked him. *Whatever, lady. That's fine.* Jack smiled and winked at her as he left. *I wouldn't have liked you either.*

Outside the sky was still blue but the air was cooler. Jack paused to wind his scarf on. Then he checked the contents of the small white envelope and slipped it into his inside coat pocket. He tried not to spend it too quickly in his head, but half was gone before he knew it.

A white BMW with a rusty scratch in its bonnet pulled into the drive and a young woman got out. She stood beside the car a moment, talking to the driver through the window. Jack guessed it was Annabelle's daughter. He walked slowly towards her.

'Don't worry, I won't tell her anything,' the teenager said. She crossed her arms and shook her head. Her voice was whiny and her manner insolent. She looked about eighteen or nineteen. Annabelle must have been young when she had her. The girl wore a short denim skirt revealing too much leg and a white sleeveless top that revealed too much of everything else. There was a faded denim jacket in her hand. Obviously she did not feel the cold.

Bracelets jingled up and down her arms as she continued to speak. 'All right, all right! I said I wouldn't, didn't I? God!'

She leaned over and gave a reluctant kiss to the driver. Then she marched down the driveway, her ponytail bouncing with fury.

She stopped in front of Jack. 'Who are you?' she snapped.

'I'm the gas man.'

She eyed him suspiciously. 'Who let you in?'

Jack saw Annabelle in the girl's eyes and in the shape of her forehead and chin. In fact, her whole face was her mother's. The body was almost there, too. Whatever her father had passed on had merely held the door open.

'Your grandfather asked me over for a drink,' said Jack. 'Louisa, isn't it?'

Annabelle's daughter scoffed and walked off without a word. Jack grinned. They taught them young in Double Bay.

The BMW began to back out of the drive. Jack caught a glimpse of the driver before his window wound up. He could not place the man there and then, but was sure he had seen him somewhere before. He thought about it for a moment, but nothing clicked. He struck a match and cupped his hands and lit his cigarette. Then he started off down the road. The scotch burnt in his stomach and he decided to buy himself a good meal. He tapped the envelope in his pocket. It was making him feel warm all over.

~2~

It was 9.00 a.m. Still an hour before Susko Books opened for trade. Down the front steps Jack saw somebody was already waiting for him. The man was standing beside a box that looked big enough to accommodate a bar fridge. No doubt the guy thought he was sitting on a small fortune in rare books. The early birds always did.

'Morning!'

Jack nodded hello. He slipped the key into the front door. 'We actually open at ten,' he said.

'Oh.' The guy looked lost for a moment. He was in his seventies, built small and thin, looked about as heavy as a copy of *War and Peace*. The skin on his face was like rice paper, and he had blotchy cheeks and a long nose. His hair was white and oily and all short back and sides. He wore a grey parka and a red flannelette shirt, buttoned to the neck and tucked into light blue slacks pulled up high and belted tight. There was no way a draught was going to get anywhere near this boy's kidneys.

The old guy patted his box. 'Any chance you can take a look? You see my son dropped me off in the car, and ...' His wet eyes pleaded. Then he smiled, changed his mind and decided to tempt rather than beg. 'Got some real beauties in here!'

Jack knew he was going to let him in. Though on the outside he might appear cool, the second-hand book dealer could never resist a box of books. The chance of that rare, elusive first edition, worth three grand, picked up for three bucks. It was a curse.

'Come in,' said Jack.

'I'll just need a hand, if you don't mind ... '

Jack walked across to the counter and put his coffee down. Maybe there was an Edward Kass or two in there? He helped the man drag the box over. It weighed a ton. Jack had a look inside.

'What do you reckon?'

All Jack could see were copies of *Reader's Digest*. 'Is your son picking you up again in the car?'

'Eh?'

'I don't buy magazines.'

'Oh.' The old man's hand went to his chin. Then he reached into the box and began to pull the copies of *Reader's Digest* out. 'Hang on, there's books in here, too! My wife packed the bloody thing, you just can't see them. Take a look!'

Soon they were piled over the concrete floor of Susko Books. Reluctantly, Jack crouched down and went through them: rejects on the right, offers on the left. Most went on the right. But he did manage to find a few things worth keeping: half-a-dozen Beatrix Potter books; a hardcover book on embroidery; a 1982 edition of the *Macquarie Dictionary of Australian Quotations*; *Gemstones of the World* by Walter Schumann; *Let's Speak French* by The Commonwealth Office of Education, Sydney; Patrick O'Brien's *Picasso*; *The Eye of the Storm* by Patrick White; a 1982 edition of the *Collins English Dictionary*; *Foucault's Pendulum* by Umberto Eco; and *The Complete Book of Flower Preservation* by Geneal Condon.

'Forty dollars,' said Jack.

It was clear from the look on the old man's face that this was not the amount he had confidently predicted to his wife and son.

'What about the rest?'

'Sorry. Can't use it.'

'Not at all?'

Jack shook his head. 'Not if you gave it to me for free.'

'I just can't believe it.'

They never could. And they always took it personally, as though Jack were passing judgement on what they had chosen to read. He supposed he was. It was one of the few perks of the job. But it was just a small God complex, nothing too serious. It did not affect the fate of nations.

'I can give you a hand up the stairs if you want.'

Jack locked the front door and pulled the *Yellow Pages* out
from a dented, grey filing cabinet behind the counter. Apart
from the shelving, the only other furniture in the shop
included a cheap pinewood chair, a small trestle table that
served as a desk, a set of drawers tucked in underneath, and
a tall free-standing lamp that he had inherited from the last
business that occupied the premises. 'Antique World' had
not lasted long and in the end made a quick, overnight exit,
leaving a good portion of rent unpaid. Jack moved in cheaply
because nobody wanted basement premises in the city: apart
from porn operators, who did not rely on display windows
so much for their trade. But 'Serious Titillation' was already
there, and had been for years, right above the basement
site. With its bright yellow sign and bright yellow façade,
it deflected a lot of attention away from Susko Books. But
that was okay. On some days there was a little bit of flow-on
traffic. Always the odd customer who came in accidentally
and was convinced to buy a copy of *The Story of O*.

Jack flipped through the *Yellow Pages* until he got to
Books — Secondhand & / or Antiquarian. He dropped a pen into
the spine. He figured he would let his fingers do the walking.
This was going to be the easiest money he had ever made.

The phone on the counter began to ring. Jack drank some
coffee before answering.

'Susko Books.'

'Yeah, I was wondering if you had a copy of a particular
book.'

'What's the title?'

'It's by a guy called Edward Kass.'

'Kass?'

'Yeah. Got anything by him?'

Jack sipped his coffee again. It was a little too early for coincidences. 'Not sure,' he said. 'Let me check.' He held the phone for half a minute. Then: 'Is that K, A, double S?'

'Yeah, that's right. I'll take everything you got.'

'Hang on.'

Jack put the phone down. He drank some more coffee. He did not feel so good. Kasprowicz might have twenty people out there working for him, all over the country. It was clear the old man did not play tiddlywinks.

'I've got two Edward Kass books,' said Jack. 'A couple of copies of *Simply Even*. Want me to hold them for you?'

'I'll be there in half an hour.'

'No problem. What's the name?'

There was a spilt-second pause. 'Steve.'

'Surname?'

'What do you want that for?'

Jack grinned. 'Got a phone number?'

'I said I'd be there in half an hour.'

'No worries.' Jack glanced at the clock on the wall behind him. 'So you're a fan of this Kass then?'

Another pause. 'They're not for me.'

'Oh. Present for someone?'

'Yeah, that's it, a present. For my niece. She reads a lot.'

'That's great. Why does she need two copies of the same book?'

A couple of moments rowed by. 'I got *two* nieces,' the man said. 'Twins.'

'That's nice, Uncle Steve,' said Jack. 'The books are one hundred dollars each.'

'A hundred bucks! You're joking.'

'Don't waste a trip down if you don't believe me.'

'Yeah? Well, fuck you then.' The man hung up.

Jack finished his coffee. So others were out there, snatching at Kasprowicz's fifty-dollar bills. He needed to find thirteen more copies if he was to keep his advance. Maybe it was not going to be as easy as he first thought.

The old guy really wanted those books. Jack knew collectors could be eccentric, obsessed and sometimes plain crazy, but Kasprowicz was not any of these. He was calm and sure of himself. He was a man used to the driver's seat. And he knew which way the numbers went, like an abacus. So what was it with this Edward Kass?

The sun was low, hidden behind the city's cold steel buildings. So far it had been the warmest winter on record, but that was over now. Today something had shifted. Though it was bright and clear and dry, everything was as sharp as broken glass. The wind blew, cold enough to snap-freeze a two-year-old's runny nose.

Jack stepped on his cigarette. The rear door at Susko Books opened onto Market Row, a narrow lane just wide enough for council garbage trucks to pass. Jack could smoke there with the door open and still see into the shop. A small alcove shielded him from rain and wind. Some mornings he found people asleep there. Often he had to sweep syringes away, or move old blankets and cardboard boxes so that he could open the door. This morning there was a twisted-up wire coathanger on the ground. Somebody must have tried their luck at free parking. Somebody else must have tried their luck for a free car. Lots happened down narrow city lanes at night.

Jack was thinking about places where he could not afford to live. Houses he could not afford to buy. Annabelle Kasprowicz. But too much thinking was not healthy. Especially when it had nothing to do with nothing. It deserved a government health warning. Jack went back inside and locked the door.

He made a few calls. None of the people he spoke with took much notice of his request for books by Edward Kass. Most just said, *Come and have a look, I wouldn't have a clue what we had.* Maybe Kasprowicz had not hired too many more people after all? Maybe just one or two? Or maybe the phone call earlier had really been a coincidence? Either way, Jack decided to close the shop for a couple of hours and see what he could find. Fifty bucks was fifty bucks.

He began with the eastern suburbs. Kenneth Brown Bookseller, Surry Hills, was the first stop and a good start: one copy of *Entropy House.* Then Cassandra's Pre-Loved Books, Darlinghurst: nothing. Phrase and Fable Book Basement, Woolloomooloo: nothing. Bentley's Book Bonanza, Kings Cross: one copy of *The Cull.* Berlichingen Books, Paddington: nothing. Upstairs, Turn Left Books, Edgecliff: nothing. Numerous Editions, Bondi Junction: nothing. Peter's Book Exchange, Bondi Junction: nothing. Rare Books and Music and Stuff, Randwick: nothing. Over three hours of his time, nearly thirty dollars in cab fares, and only two Edward Kass books and an eye-strain headache to show for it. Plus a greasy falafel roll he ate for lunch was taking its sweet goddamn time through his alimentary canal. Pick a good mood: Jack Susko was not in it.

He headed out to Glebe anyway. One last try for the afternoon. Jack knew the guy who ran a place called Jack and the Bookstalk. His name was Chester Sinclair. He had used Jack and the Bookstalk without telling Jack he had stolen his idea. Sinclair was that kind of guy.

He always wore tracksuit pants that sagged under the weight of keys, wallet, mobile phone and God knows what else. Sometimes he wore leather lace-up shoes with the tracksuit pants, the elastic cuffs gripping high up his ankles, revealing white socks that had turned grey with despair. He was in his forties, tall but soft in the gut. He had wispy blonde hair that curled a little around his ears and gave him a boyish look. Combined with his blue eyes, there was a suggestion that he might have surfed once upon a time, though this was very far from the truth. He was pale like an unripe strawberry and sweaty all over. And always grinning, always smiling, like he knew something that you were dying to know and there was no way he was ever going to tell you what it was. He was cheap and would not hesitate to confuse old ladies with their change. He never wrote prices on his books but made them up at the counter after he had sized up the customer. He did not possess a healthy aura.

Jack's worry was that Chester would sniff out that the Kass books might be worth something. With the right kind of breeze, the man could smell Monopoly money buried at the South Pole.

Jack and the Bookstalk was located in an old warehouse building just off Glebe Point Road, its grey rendered façade peeling with fifty years' worth of advertising posters. It had once been a smash repair business: oil stains were still visible on the concrete floor. The musty, damp air carried a whiff of resin and paint and petrol. Inside was chaos. There was a ground floor and mezzanine level, both sick with books. They were crammed onto exhausted shelves and piled on the floor like war dead after an offensive. Everything blended into the colour of mulch. It was a place where you could easily go insane.

It was colder inside than out on the street. Jack saw Chester at the front counter, sorting through papers. He wore a pink, long-sleeve polo top and a navy blue muffler, the collar up high around his neck. Jack could hear a fan blowing air. Music drifted softly from a radio somewhere.

'Here he is,' said Chester when he saw Jack. 'The man himself.'

Jack nodded. 'Mr Sinclair.'

'Taking the afternoon off, I see.'

'Nothing gets by you. You're amazing.'

Chester shook his head and tapped a bundle of papers on the counter. He had soft, pale hands, with fingers that started wide at the base but then tapered into thin ends, crowned with long, narrow fingernails. He put the papers down and reached under the counter for a tube of moisturiser. He squirted a good amount in the palm of his hand and proceeded to rub the moisturiser in. His hands writhed together obscenely.

Jack tried not to listen to the sound they made. 'Did you get my message?' he asked.

'Yes I did. And I found a few copies, too. Four in fact. That make you happy?'

'How did you find them in all this?'

'There's a system in operation here, *compadre*. Just 'cause you can't see it.' Chester looked down at his hands as he massaged in between his fingers with his thumb.

'I wouldn't want to go blind with the brilliance of it,' said Jack.

'Genius is like that.' Chester's grin tucked into his right cheek. 'So, who's this Edward Kass then?'

Jack picked up a book from the counter: *The Book of Miracles—How to get to Heaven AND make a Profit!* 'He's a poet,' he answered, dropping the book.

'Famous?'

'Unhappy.'

'But, of course. There's no money in poetry.' Chester began searching under the counter. 'They're down here somewhere, hang on.'

A young guy came in the front door. He wore black jeans, a black denim jacket, a red-and-black striped scarf and a tight black knitted beanie. A dark green knapsack was hooked over his shoulder. He was as skinny as an incense stick. Jack guessed a university student: his face was white and pimply and wore all the burden of global injustices perpetrated by multinational companies.

'You work here?' he asked Jack.

'No.'

Chester stood up. He put the Edward Kass books onto the counter. 'Can I help you?' he asked in a stern voice.

'Have you got a philosophy section?'

Chester pointed toward the back of the shop. 'Straight ahead, on your left. And what's there is what I've got so don't ask me for anything.'

'Right.' The kid gave a pained look and walked off, shaking his head.

'Now, Mr Susko.' Chester leaned on the counter and spread his grin to both cheeks. 'You know, there was a guy in here yesterday asking for the very same author. Bit of a coincidence. I was tempted to sell, I have to tell you. A man's got to eat. But it wouldn't have been too professional of me, would it?'

'Your integrity has always been impeccable.'

'That's what I wanted to hear.' Chester picked up one of the books and flicked through the pages. Jack leaned on the counter with both elbows.

'When you're ready, Chester,' he said, looking down at the scratches in the wood.

'I'm thinking.'

'Don't hurt yourself.'

'So who was this other guy then?'

Jack looked up and sighed and tried to look bored. 'How the hell would I know?'

'I can smell something that's all.' Chester scratched an armpit. 'Why do you want 'em?'

'I got a collector.'

'What are you getting?'

'Do you think I'm going to retire on the sale of four books of poetry? It's not fucking *Lolita*, signed by Nabokov and dedicated to Graham Greene.'

Chester scratched his other armpit. 'Ten bucks each.'

'Come on, Sinclair. This isn't Sotheby's.'

'Take it or leave it.'

'Leave it,' said Jack. He turned to go.

'Thirty bucks for the lot.'

Jack pulled out his wallet. 'Don't spend it all on jelly beans.'

Back in the city, there was a note pushed in under the door of Susko Books. It was from Annabelle Kasprowicz.

I waited. Interesting concept of running a business. I'll try tomorrow. 2pm.

It was all happening today. Jack held the note to his nose. Her pricey perfume was all over it. He folded the note and put it in his coat pocket. Nothing like having something to look forward to.

~ *3* ~

ANOTHER COOL MORNING. On the bus people sat a little hunched over, sniffing and sneezing into tissues and handkerchiefs. In the city streets they pulled their collars up and leaned into the cold. The sky was clear but looked to be coming down with something: watery clouds soaked the horizon. Down by the Queen Victoria Building, a homeless man had found a sunny spot and pulled his trouser legs up, as though he were working on a tan. He had no shoes, his ankles were swollen and he was as grimy as diesel exhaust. Jack dropped a couple of dollars in his paper cup. The authorities said not to give the homeless money because they only spent it on booze. Better than Jack taking the guy home and giving him a bath.

Susko Books was an icebox. Being underground kept it cool in summer, but winter was a whole other disaster. Two fan-forced heaters made as much difference as striking a match. The best Jack could do was play a little smoky jazz or blues on the stereo and hope the shop at least sounded warmer. Miles Davis and Muddy Waters had worked overtime this winter. No doubt they would soon ask for a raise.

It was 10.30 a.m. Jack had placed one of the heaters behind the counter and he sat beside it, pretending he was warm. He was on the net, doing a search on Edward Kass. He was trying hard not to think too much about Annabelle Kasprowicz and their afternoon rendezvous. He was not doing a very good job. Even a monkey could tell she was only coming to see Jack because of her father, but this did not prevent fantastic thoughts rising in his mind. Every time he entertained the idea that she had a thing for him, he had to step outside and smoke a cigarette and talk himself out of it. The cigarettes had not helped his nervous stomach. And now the net was inducing its own brand of nausea.

There were over 382,000 references to Edward Kass. So far, none were about the poet. He found an Edward Kass who had written a comparative empirical analysis of theoretical formulations of distrust. He found an Edward Kass who had written a paper titled: *Are Negotiators Overly Optimistic After All? It Depends on the Question and the Negotiation Structure.* He found an Edward Kass who was a specialist in urinary tract infections and one who was married to a famous mountain climber. There was an Edward Kass mentioned in the minutes of the 2002 annual meeting of the Stirk Group of Companies. A couple of people had even won an Edward Kass Award. But still no poet.

Jack could not take anymore. He double-clicked one last reference. A black-and-white photograph appeared on the screen: *Edward Kass, poet (b.1934)*. It was a grainy headshot, slightly out of focus. Kass wore a heavy, large-collared coat and a striped scarf. There was no date but it looked like a reject passport photo from the 1950s. He had a long rectangular face, the skin drawn drum-tight over bones that appeared to have been sculpted with a Stanley knife. His hair was receding and cut short. Kass might have been handsome from another angle but the photographer had not been able to find it. He had a strong straight nose and ears set low on his head. His eyes were cast down, sunk deep in the sockets and crowned with heavy brows that made them look bruised. His fleshy lips were parted as though he were about to say something to himself. The light caught him like grey rain from an Eastern European cloud. Sadness seemed to drizzle all over him.

Time might pass but Edward Kass would remain vulnerable forever, caught just like this. Jack was sorry for him. Never put your dukes down, even outside the ring. There was always somebody in the crowd ready with a king hit.

Below the photograph there was a list of publications and links to reviews in newspapers and literary journals. Biographical details repeated what Jack already knew. That was about it. Hammond Kasprowicz's interest in the man remained a mystery. Jack was tempted to keep searching but had to get some food. He did not want his stomach rumbling in front of Annabelle Kasprowicz. He printed off the photograph and smoked another cigarette while he waited.

She was wearing a dark brown gypsy skirt and red leather cowboy boots. They were slightly worn, no doubt a favourite pair, purchased on an unforgettable trip to Mexico. The rest of her was kept warm by a coffee-bean cashmere turtleneck that did everything it could to draw attention to her physiology. There was not a straight line anywhere. Long red earrings flashed through her hair. She took off her sunglasses and pushed them into a large leather shoulder bag worth more than Jack's architecture and design section when it was new. She was an hour and a half late but did not look like she was going to apologise.

'It's neat,' she said as she looked around Susko Books.

'I have tendencies.'

'I see.'

She walked over to the counter and put her bag down. She looked around some more. Muddy Waters sang: *You're gonna need my help I said.* Jack put his hands in his pockets. She smelt like cinnamon.

'Are you cold?' he asked.

'No, not at all.'

'My heating is on holiday.'

A smile came and went like a blink.

'Far north Queensland,' said Jack, hoping for more.

Her face remained serious. 'Can you tell me what my father is paying you for, exactly?'

'Want to grab some coffee? Tea? Smoked salmon bagel?

There's a nice café up the road.'

She shook her head. 'I'd rather you answered my question.'

'Why didn't you just ask your father?'

'My father ...' she began, but pulled herself up. She looked down at her boots. 'I know he's after some books by Edward Kass. Did he tell you why he wanted them?'

'No. Why?'

'Are you sure?'

Jack frowned. 'I'm sure.'

'I just thought that ... he might have mentioned something. He didn't say anything then?'

'Why don't you tell me something?'

Annabelle hesitated a moment. 'It's not the first time I've caught him buying Edward Kass books.'

'Caught him?'

'Discovered them in his possession.'

'I didn't know they were illegal.'

Annabelle looked away. Little Walter's harmonica moaned. Muddy sang. *Gonna need my help I said.*

'Does your father know Edward Kass?' asked Jack.

Annabelle reached into her bag and pulled out a small black case. Inside were some reading glasses with narrow rectangular frames and pale pink arms. The lenses were slightly tinted. They suited her. No doubt everything suited her. She slid them on and walked over to one of the bookshelves.

'Susko,' she said, running her finger down the line of books. 'That's a strange name, isn't it?'

'Should've seen what it was before I changed it.'

She looked up, her finger stopped on a book.

'Jones,' said Jack and shook his head in despair. Her smile lasted longer this time.

'Jack Jones does have a certain ring to it,' she said, returning her attention to the book spines. 'You could have called yourself Jay Jay.'

Jack came out from behind the counter. He leaned against it, crossed his arms over his chest. 'What about Kasprowicz? Bet you've had fun spelling that.'

'Sure have,' she said, coolly. 'It cashes all the cheques.'

'That's handy. Polish?'

'Very good, Jay Jay. My mother hated it and never took it as her own. She stayed Temple. Except when she signed the cheques.'

Jack walked over to the bookcases. He could see Annabelle through the gaps on the shelf. Her cowboy boots clicked across the polished concrete floor. Muddy started the riff to 'Whiskey Blues'.

'Australia via ... ?'

'London,' she said. 'The old story, running away from the Nazis. Easy when you're loaded.'

'What isn't?'

'Love.'

'Let me guess. Your favourite Beatle was Paul.'

She did not reply. Jack tried again. 'So who's Edward Kass?'

Annabelle walked around the end of the aisle. She stopped beside Jack and passed him a book.

'This looks interesting. Do I get a discount?' Jack took the book without looking at it.

Annabelle lingered beside him. 'He's my uncle,' she said. 'On my father's side.'

The door to Susko Books swung open and a customer entered. Cold air rushed down the steps: dead leaves and a page of soiled newspaper blew into the shop. Jack looked around to see who had come in. A man was closing the door behind him.

Annabelle gathered her bag off the counter. When she turned towards the front door she froze.

The guy was grinning like a cartoon cat. He had a lean, tanned face, all blue-eyed and square-jawed. Except the tan looked a little *tandoori* to Jack. His straw-coloured hair was short and thinning, styled to look like all he ever did was run his hand through it, casually. A tight little paunch said that he was not as young as he wanted to look. He had splashed on about a hundred bucks' worth of aftershave. He wore faded blue designer jeans, pale yellow leather slip-ons, and a loose grey blazer over a white T-shirt and black knitted vest. Overall, he seemed pretty fit. He had a couple of inches on Jack, both up and sideways. A BMW key ring dangled between the fingers of his clenched right hand.

Jack recognised him. It was the guy he had seen in the car with Louisa at Kasprowicz's house.

'Hello, Annabelle,' he said, still grinning. His teeth were as white as cream cheese. 'Fancy seeing you here.'

Annabelle looped an arm through her bag. 'I suppose you expect me to believe it's a coincidence.' Her voice was cold. 'Leave me alone, Ian.'

Ian walked towards her. He jingled the keys in his hand. 'I was driving past before and saw you come in. Thought we could have a coffee.'

'You're joking.'

'You know I never joke, Annabelle.' He turned to Jack.

'You got to watch this one. Needs a tight leash.' His voice turned slimy, like warm suntan lotion. 'Yep, a real tight leash.'

'Fuck you,' said Annabelle. She pushed past him to the door. Ian smiled as he watched her disappear up the steps.

'You need some help?' said Jack.

The man's smile dissolved. He ran a hand through his hair, walked over and put his finger in Jack's airspace. 'Keep away from my fucking wife.'

Two seconds went past as Jack considered his next move. Two seconds too long. The man shot a dirty right fist into Jack's stomach, BMW keys and all. He stepped back. All the air inside Jack blew out fast enough to break the sound barrier. He moaned and doubled over. He tried to suck air back into his lungs but they had collapsed like a beginner's soufflé. The man went to the nearest bookcase and began to pull all the books off it. They hit the floor like a net full of wet fish. When he had finished, he gave Jack a parting knee to the ribs.

Business was slow that day. Nobody came in and saw Jack crawl over behind the counter and lift himself up into a chair. Nobody got him a couple of aspirins and a glass of water, or a stiff drink and a cigarette. Nobody helped him clear up the mess. And nobody made him chicken soup that night either.

But that was okay. Jack Susko could take care of himself.

~4~

LOIS HAD APPEARED IN THE LANE behind Susko Books about six months ago. Her right paw was off-white, like a dirty sock, the rest of her was a cheap, stripy ginger. Her ears were stubby and her tail was too long. Just a run-of-the-mill short hair, but she flounced around like Marlene Dietrich. No name, no past, and nothing to lose. A free agent with time on her paws. Jack made the mistake of tossing her some bacon out of his breakfast roll: after that, she was there every morning. He could not remember what had possessed him to take her home. She was a bedraggled thing, with no breeding or manners. She had the gall to refuse tinned pet food. But Jack could not deny there was something about her. He thought it was style. He never guessed that it was trouble.

It was a little before 6.00 a.m. Jack pushed Lois off his head and got up.

In the lounge room he turned on the heater. Lois stood in front of it and waited for the warm air to start blowing. Their ground-floor flat in Leinster Street, Paddington, was comfortable, but cold in winter. It was part of a large, double-fronted terrace that did not receive a lot of natural light. The last time it had received anything was a paint job in 1955. Its main features were a shabby ambience, high moulded ceilings and some fancy ironwork. It was apparently a fine example of the architecture of its day. Considering the rent for all this unique charm, Jack probably should have paid it more attention.

He sat down in his Eames lounge chair and pulled on a pair of socks. Along with his small collection of blues and jazz vinyl, the chair was his prize possession, a 1970s number 670 that he bought at a garage sale last year while trawling for books. It was missing its base and the footrest, and the leather had a couple of scratches in it, but for seventy-five dollars he could not believe his luck. He happily spent five hundred getting it repaired. It was the most comfortable chair in the universe. Jack yawned. Maybe he should sit in it all day.

He went into the kitchen and poured a glass of water, dropped a Berocca into it and lit a cigarette while the thing fizzed. Normally he would wait until later for his first cigarette. Each day he had been trying to beat the previous day's time, even if only by a minute. He was getting close to 8.00 a.m. But not today. Jack did not feel so good. He struck a match and drew deeply.

The damp Saturday morning streets were empty, except for some late-night boys and girls huddled under leaky awnings. They shivered, looked up and down the street, and silently wondered what to do. A few cabs drove by, searching for a last fare. Walk signals ticked loudly at intersections and bins overflowed with rubbish. Everything seemed to be suffering from a mild hangover, the sky, the buildings, even the trees. Rain drifted down in a grey mist.

Jack walked along Oxford Street. *Punched in the gut*. He felt the bruise to his ego. The worst thing about a sucker punch was the thinking afterwards: you should have done this, you should have done that. And the whole time knowing you had done nothing.

In the city he bought the weekend paper and a pack of cigarettes. He stopped at a small café in the Strand Arcade. It was a warm, timber-lined place with a few tables on one side and a row of booths on the other. Framed reproductions of old coffee and tea advertisements hung on the walls. Jack removed his coat and scarf and slipped into one of the booths. The waitress came over to take his order. Her honey blonde hair was done up in a loose bun at the back of her head. She was young and plump, her brown eyes were bright and her cheeks rosy. She made Jack feel a little better. He ordered a ham-and-cheese croissant and a long black.

A story on page four of the paper caught his eye. It was about a GP who had been supplying his receptionist with drugs. After everybody went home they liked to stay behind in the surgery and relax together, talk a bit and pop a few pills. Have some fun. Make a couple of home movies if they felt like it. Everything was going fine until one found its way onto the net. It was popular with a lot of people but none of them worked for the Medical Association of New South Wales.

Doctor Ian Durst. The name flashed into Jack's mind. The newspaper story had reminded him of a similar episode about five or six months ago, involving Mr Fake Tan of the Sucker Punches, formerly Doctor Ian Durst, gynaecologist, Double Bay. He had been struck from the medical register after a sex, drugs and money scandal. It was on the evening news: his photograph had been in the papers. That was why Jack thought he had seen Durst before, when he glimpsed his face in the car in Kasprowicz's driveway.

Durst. He said the name in a low voice. It sounded like a town in Austria. Or a type of sausage. *Son of a bitch.*

Jack paid for breakfast. It was nearly 8.30 a.m. Outside, the drizzly rain had stopped but the wind had picked up and whipped around in annoying gusts. Traffic was quickly filling the streets as Jack hurried on to Susko Books. He wanted to call Brendan MacAllister before opening up. Jack's former boss at *MacAllister's Old Books* knew a little something about everything that went on in old Sydney Town.

'Hello?'

'It's Jack.'

A pause. 'Jack?' MacAllister put on an exaggerated English accent. 'I am sorry, but I do not believe I know anybody by that name.'

'Like that, is it?' said Jack.

'I am sorry, sir, but I suspect that you may have dialled the wrong number.'

'I suppose I'll have to send you a written apology before you'll speak to me?'

MacAllister laughed. 'You can write?'

'You can read?'

Brendan MacAllister was a big man: fifty-five and fit, with dark red hair everywhere except his scalp. Handsome in a bald, bristly kind of way. His laugh was deep and resonant. Cups and cutlery shook if he happened to be at a table when something struck him as funny.

'Nice of you to call,' said MacAllister. 'I thought you were dead.'

'It's been a busy couple of months.'

'Yeah, yeah.' Then in a Scottish accent: 'Did I not treat you like a son?'

'I was an abused child, your Honour.'

'Oh, that's why you're ringing: blackmail. How much?'

'Hundred thousand ought to keep me quiet.'

'Sure, sure. Cheque okay?'

'Only if it's in a bag with the cash.'

'Funny bastard. Hang on ...'

Jack waited. He flicked through a pile of mail on the counter. He could hear MacAllister calling out to his wife.

'Right,' he said, back on the phone. 'My coffee shall be here directly.'

'How's Denise?'

'Demanding as ever. What's new with you?'

'I'm getting married.'

MacAllister grunted. 'Really? What's her name?'

'Annabelle Kasprowicz.'

'A millionaire's daughter, no less! I presume you've met the father-in-law.'

'A gentleman and a scholar.'

'In the fifth rung of hell.'

'Know him well?'

'Used to be a regular. World War II stuff. Especially keen on anything Nazi. Funny, being Jewish, family run out of Poland, all that. Sold him some diaries by an SS man last year. Didn't even want to bargain.'

Jack tapped the counter with the edge of an envelope. 'What do you know about his brother, Edward Kass?'

MacAllister slurped some coffee. 'Renowned poet. Recluse. Broke. And judging by his poetry, pretty pissed off about it.'

'Money the family rift then?'

'The perennial rich bastards' classic. Back in the seventies Edward took big brother Hammond to court over the family millions. He didn't get any.'

'Nothing?'

'Plus zero. You know mamma and papa Kasprowicz actually used to live in the same street as my parents, back in the fifties.'

'Anything else, apart from the court case?'

'A few days after the trial, Kass assaulted Kasprowicz with a fucking lamp. Hammond had to go to hospital, I don't know, stitches to the head, concussion, that sort of thing. And Kass got a suspended sentence. Aggravated assault or something. Or did I get that from the television?'

'Nice family.' Jack picked up a pen and started doodling on the back of the envelope. 'And now, years later, Kasprowicz is after as many copies of his brother's books as he can get his hands on.'

'That's what he's after?'

'Yep.'

MacAllister scoffed. 'The rich are weird.' He drank more coffee. 'Is he paying well? Just take his money and don't worry about it too much.'

Jack coloured in a rectangle but went over the edge and had to turn it into a square. 'Something else,' he said. 'What can you tell me about Ian Durst?'

'The famous gynaecologist? Jesus, you're right in there, aren't you?'

'I remember he got done for something last year.'

'You know he's Annabelle Kasprowicz's husband, don't you? Or ex, I'm not sure if they're divorced.'

'I don't think she likes him anymore.'

'Why would she?' said MacAllister. 'He's the dirtiest dog in the pound.'

'What happened?'

'The usual. Champagne, cocaine, so and so's perfect-breasted wife and her blonde best friend, the handsome doctor with hands the devil gave him in a special deal, and all after-hours in the surgery rooms. They've got those stirrups, you see.'

'Nice.'

'Beautiful. I've got some myself!'

Jack wrote *DURST* on the envelope and then scribbled it out. 'The good doctor spent all day looking between rich women's legs,' he said. 'Maybe in the end it just drove him a little crazy.'

'Having too much fun. And you know what happens when you have too much fun.' MacAllister switched to a Scottish accent again. 'My dear old mother used to say, *Where laughter starts, tears are sure to follow.*'

'What was the scandal?'

'Well, they were having so much fun they stopped thinking altogether. They threw the colours in with the whites and suddenly everything turned grey,' said MacAllister. 'Where there's sex and drugs, there's always money. Seems the blonde knew a banker who knew a lawyer who knew the wife of a CEO who bought some shares and made some quick dividends. Too quick.'

'Patience is a virtue.'

'The whole thing was bent like a giant banana. And it all came out because a monkey called Durst got caught in a cubicle bending over a high-heeled babe with a hundred-dollar roll up her nose and his smooth hand down her pants. And then they all had none.'

'Anyone else get into trouble?'

'Businessmen are allowed to play, but not doctors. Durst was the only one who ended up with none. And he'd actually made his money from working. The rest couldn't lose it if they dropped it out of a plane over the Pacific Ocean in a hurricane.'

'Money clings to them like a birthmark.'

'Yeah, and they've always got one the size of a frying pan. Mine's in my crack and you can't see it with the naked eye.' MacAllister sighed. 'You know I met Durst once. Real arrogant bastard, all slicked-back hair, aftershave and perfect teeth.'

'What was he after?'

'Gift for his wife. Anniversary, I think. Kasprowicz must have suggested it because he had no idea.'

'Did he buy anything?'

'Yeah, a copy of *The Great Gatsby*. It was the only title he recognised out of my first editions. He said, oh yeah, Robert Redford wrote this. For fuck's sake!'

'Now, now, Brendan,' said Jack. 'Reserving judgements is a matter of infinite hope.'

'According to Fitzgerald.' The telephone brushed against his beard and the sound was like radio static. 'Not a bad little copy though,' he said wistfully. 'British first edition from Chatto & Windus. Okay, the dust jacket was average and the book was a bit rough round the edges, but nice for two and a half grand.'

'Thanks. You always know the good stuff. You should write a book.'

'Twenty-five years serving the rich and bored, my friend. This is nothing. Run-of-the-mill scandal. There's much, much more. If I wrote it all down it'd be longer than the *Encyclopaedia Britannica*.'

~5~

Jack spent most of Sunday afternoon in a small, musty attic room in Balmain, all spider webs and dust and dejected cardboard boxes. The deceased estate: another feature of the second-hand dealer's lot. Looking through dead people's crap, driven by the slim possibility of finding something of value.

The final haul was meagre: a small box of literary pretension from the 1950s and 1960s. *Man and His Symbols* by Jung; John Barthes' *Giles Goat Boy* and *The Sotweed Factor*; the trilogy *Nexus*, *Sexus* and *Plexus* by Henry Miller; Camus' *The Myth of Sisyphus* and Simone de Beauvoir's *The Mandarins*; *The Unquiet Grave* by Palinurus; and *Meetings with Remarkable Men* by G.I. Gurdjieff.

There was an elaborate bookplate with a striped coat of arms inside the front cover of each volume: *From the Library of Harold J. Cummins*. Obviously Harry had been all class. The books were in excellent condition. Jack wondered if he had ever actually read any of them.

Only one little volume really interested him. It was the last book he found, right at the bottom of a crumpled cardboard box, squashed under the weight of a small horde of old literary journals and magazines. Jack supposed it was not too much of a coincidence. Because trawling books was what he did, because at any given time, with any box full of books, the odds were there. That Jack had met the author's brother two days ago had nothing to do with nothing.

The front cover was dark blue. The title and the author's name were in grey typeface. Below, in the bottom third of the cover, was a reproduction of Hundertwasser's *Genesis—Pieces of Pineapple*. The strong yellows and greens seemed a little colourful for Kass. Almost humorous. It was the first copy of *Simply Even* that Jack had come across.

Inside, it was inscribed: *Dearest Harold, For all your help. With gratitude, Edward.*

Jack directed the taxi straight over to Susko Books so that he could dump the box and not have to worry about lugging it there in the morning. The city was empty and spacious. A calm had settled along with the drizzle. It looked clean in the pearly afternoon light. This was how Jack liked it best. The city in winter. Red wine weather. He remembered there was a bottle of cheap Shiraz under the counter at the shop.

Apart from a few people waiting for buses, York Street was deserted. Jack got out of the taxi and took his box from the back seat. As he crossed the road he heard the flags on top of the Queen Victoria Building snapping in the wind, their cables ringing out against the poles like thin, erratic bells. He glanced at the Town Hall clock. Just after 4.00 p.m.

He opened the front door to Susko Books and stepped inside. The light was metallic, blue-grey, but soft too, regardless of the cold. Jack left the lights off. He put the box on the counter and switched on the heater by his desk. From a drawer he took out an aluminium ashtray and from under the counter the bottle of Shiraz.

He took the Edward Kass book from the box and pressed play on the stereo. *Sketches of Spain* drifted into the shop like a warm desert wind. It reminded Jack that he still had not read *Don Quixote*.

He sat down at his desk, poured wine into a glass and lit a cigarette. He opened *Simply Even* at random. Page 12.

GREEK TRAGEDY

Close me to your breast.

Soothe the broken rhythm
Of my heartbeat
That has reduced me to a wreck
Of ribs upon the rocks.

I can no longer grip
This oily chain

Of endless days.

My every sweetness
Is swirled away.

Jack brushed some ash from the page. He flipped through the book again. Page 36.

LINE THEORY

You slink away
adjusted
by a hammer blow.

A charred bud
marks your hand. Tomorrow
again
the wet day of your conception.

Remember, alive
you never leave
anything behind.

So much for the bright cover.

The phone rang. Jack put the book down, went to the counter and answered.

'Susko Books.'

'Jack?'

It was Annabelle Kasprowicz.

'Speaking.'

'Oh, it's you. I wasn't sure if anybody else worked there.'

Jack leaned against the counter. 'Well, there's Carlos,' he said. 'But he never answers the damn phone. I'm thinking about sending him back to Costa Rica.'

Annabelle Kasprowicz did not laugh but she might have smiled. 'I tried your home but there was no answer.'

Jack swapped the receiver to his other ear. He glanced at the clock on the wall behind him. 'What can I do for you at a quarter past four on a Sunday afternoon when I shouldn't even be here?'

'Are you closed?'

'Only for the masses, Ms Kasprowicz.'

'Please, call me Annabelle.'

'Sure.' Jack heard the click of a lighter and a quick sharp breath.

'This is a bit awkward. But ... well, I heard about what happened on Friday. After I left. I just wanted to apologise. Are you all right?'

Jack rubbed the edge of the counter with a thumb. Durst must have told her. 'It wasn't your fault,' he said.

'Well, yes it was, sort of. You see—' She pulled herself up. 'Anyway, I'm sorry. I stormed out and didn't even say goodbye.'

Jack tucked the phone into his chin and reached over for the glass of wine on the desk. 'Bit of bad luck he saw you come in. That's all.'

She did not reply. The line droned for a moment.

'Unlucky coincidence.'

'Yes,' said Annabelle, as though she were talking to herself. Then she took a deep breath. 'Our divorce comes through next month,' she said, raising her voice a little. 'The official end. Of course, he wants us to get back together.'

'Right.' Jack put the wineglass down and picked up his burning cigarette. He thought about Ian Durst. He pictured Annabelle Kasprowicz with Ian Durst. He said nothing.

'Listen,' she said, 'I feel awful about what happened. I was hoping you might let me make it up to you. Lunch, tomorrow?'

'Well, I do have this little business to run.'

'Okay then, what about dinner?'

'Sure.'

'Here, about seven?'

'At your place?' The words came out too quickly.

'Yes, unless you'd prefer somewhere else.'

'No, that's fine. I mean, whatever you like. You don't have to go to any trouble.'

'Don't you think I can cook?'

Jack grinned. 'I've got no idea.'

Annabelle blew smoke down the line. 'My father won't be here. He's away. Business.'

It threw him. A couple of seconds passed before he managed a squeaky, 'Okay.' What did she mean? He was already trying to remember her tone, but the words had faded too quickly. He waited for her to say something else, to give him a clue. She said nothing. The pause was pregnant with triplets.

'Seven o'clock then?' she said.

This time Jack was sure she was smiling.

~6~

OLD MAN TIME WAS A SMART-ARSE. You wanted it slow, he gave it fast. You wanted it fast, he gave it slow. Today, Jack wanted it fast. So Monday dragged like it had rolled an ankle.

By noon, Susko Books had seen just three people, not including Jack or his reflection in the front-door glass when he walked over and looked up the stairs at the street. Two pissed-off couriers came in asking for directions and a shoplifter tried to offload some books. It was the same guy he had seen the week before. A hard worker but not particularly bright. He stole the books from two doors down—a large retail bookshop called *Index*—and then walked straight over to Jack's and tried to sell them. He even left the price stickers on, so that Jack could see he was getting a great deal. The man was wiry and wrinkled and looked like a sad old jockey with no horse left to ride. He had small, pale blue eyes that glistened like he had just swallowed a shot of cheap scotch. Body odour did not appear to bother him. There was a faded blue-grey tattoo of a small bird on the back of his right hand, between the base of his thumb and forefinger. He spoke quickly and in short bursts, in a thin voice like an old woman's. The first time he came around, Jack felt sorry for the guy and gave him a few dollars for the books. It was a bad move: encouragement should be dispensed with caution, like painkillers. And so here he was again this afternoon. The latest haul: half-a-dozen paperbacks, all the latest releases, and a Jeffrey Archer hardback. That he managed to shove so much down his pants deserved some kind of acknowledgement. Jack tried but could not think of a more legal use for the man's skills.

'You read a lot.'

'Nah,' the man said. 'Presents I don't want.'

'Right.'

'Fifty bucks. That's a bargain.'

Jack shook his head. 'I don't need them.'

An instant aggression prickled the air around the man. Jack remembered somebody telling him: *always watch out for the short guys.*

'Yes, you do,' said the short guy.

Jack watched him look around the shop: nobody but the two of them. What if he jumped the counter? Pulled a knife?

'Fifty bucks.'

'No,' said Jack.

The man's watery eyes were a little narrower now. He glanced towards the front door, then down to his right. He looked back at Jack, grinning. Slowly, he turned to his left, followed the aisle of books that led to the rear door. Craned his head, squinted at something. Nodded a couple of times, as though agreeing to buy the place.

'Okay. See you next time.' He walked out with his merchandise.

'Can't wait,' whispered Jack.

That was it until about 3.00 p.m. as far as business went. At 3.10 the mailman stuck his head inside the front door, smiled and said: 'Nothing for you today.' For some reason he had never liked Jack.

Half an hour later, the phone rang. It was Chester Sinclair.

'What?'

'I was just thinking that I should sell you the name Jack and the Bookstalk. It'd suit you more than me. Seein' as your name's Jack. How about twenty-five grand?'

'Sure. Rupees okay with you?'

'You mock me and I come with an open heart.'

'What did you find when you opened it? An IOU?'

'Boy. Somebody better get nice if they want to hear something interesting.'

'Chester, I'm busy. What do you want?'

'Nothing.'

'Right.'

'Wait!'

Jack waited.

'Well?' said Chester.

'Well what?'

'You going to say sorry and ask nicely for the information I've acquired? I'm sure you'd love it.'

'Yeah, of course.'

'It concerns your poet.'

Jack took a deep breath and forced it out through his nostrils. 'And?'

'Now I'm not sure if I should tell you.'

'Chester, I think I know why you can't get a woman.'

'Now I'm definitely not going to tell you.'

'Bye.'

'Hold it, hold it. So fucking *nasty* today.'

'Okay. You have my sincerest apologies.'

'Fine. That's all I wanted. See how easy it is to be nice?'

Jack closed his eyes and shook his head. 'And so?'

'Well, I reckon you've ripped me off. Those Kass books are pretty popular all of a sudden. First some guy, then you, and now today some lady was after them as well. She was posh, too. And she was very interested to hear about you.'

'What do you mean?'

'I told her that I'd sold my last copies and she asked who to—hang on, she said *to whom*—and I told her about you. Expect her sometime today or tomorrow.'

'Did she tell you who she was?'

'No. Wasn't bad looking though, for an older chick.' Chester paused. 'So we'll forget about the first lot, but from now on, whatever I get we split down the middle.'

'Excuse me?'

'The Kass books. You've got the contact, I'll get the merchandise. Fifty-fifty.'

'Do you think you're in a movie, Chester?'

'Hey man, I sent her over as a gesture of goodwill. Come on. This is business. We'll find more books if we're both looking.'

'How many books do you think I need?' Jack hoped his voice sounded loose and unconcerned.

'You tell me. Then I'll make you an offer you can't refuse,' said Chester with a terrible *Godfather* accent.

'Sinclair, I promise I'll keep you in mind when the Cosa Nostra approach me about heroin distribution. Okay?'

'Wait—'

Jack put the phone down. Hearing from Chester Sinclair was one of his least favourite things in the world.

It was one minute to closing time when she walked in.

'Are you still open?'

'Sorry, just locking up.' Jack finished putting his coat on.

'Oh.'

He switched off the heaters and walked over to where the lady was standing, just inside the front door. She was an older woman, maybe in her early fifties, but looked like she took care of herself. She had a broad oval face of fine pale skin, with delicate cheekbones and a high, smooth forehead. Her lips were pale too, and her mouth was wide and straight, with thin wrinkles lining the corners like apostrophes. A narrow nose with slightly flared nostrils. Her dark brown hair was shoulder length and cut in a plain bob. She had soft hazel eyes: they looked at Jack with vague trepidation.

'Sorry,' he repeated.

She remained where she was. A new wardrobe would have helped. Instead, she wore a maroon polo neck under a thick knitted cardigan of turquoise-blue and purple, with long sleeves down to her palms and large multicoloured buttons. Also a dark blue woollen skirt, stockings and brown moccasins. There was a large, brown hessian bag over her shoulder with the handle of an umbrella sticking out. It was in the shape of an English bobby's helmet. Jack would have said art teacher. Or maybe a children's book illustrator. She looked a little uptight, but he sensed there was a warm fire glowing in a back room somewhere. He bet she still loved the Rolling Stones.

'We're open again tomorrow,' said Jack. 'Ten o'clock.'

'Oh, I don't mean to hold you up.' She adjusted the bag on her shoulder. 'Can you spare five minutes? I promise I'll buy something.'

Her voice was pleasant to listen to. She enunciated every vowel like the Queen's fifth cousin by marriage.

'Okay,' he said. 'Five minutes.'

She stepped out of the way as Jack went to the door and flicked the sign over to *Closed*.

'Anything in particular you were looking for?'

'Well, I was hoping you had a poetry section.'

'Yeah.' Jack grinned. 'There's a poetry section. French surrealists?'

She laughed. 'Oh no! Thankfully I haven't been in my twenties for a long time. I was actually after some Australian poetry.'

'Right. Just down here.'

Jack showed her the section and left her to it. He walked over to his desk, opened a drawer and pulled out the Edward Kass books. He laid them on the counter in a neat fan. Then he went around to the other side and waited for the woman to finish looking.

After a couple of minutes she came back. She seemed disappointed.

'Not what you were after?'

'No,' she said. She swapped the bag to her other shoulder. 'That's all you have?'

'Pretty much. Oh, I've got these too, but they're for a customer.' Jack moved so that the woman could see. 'He's a wealthy collector. My first one. Ever.'

She looked. Her hairline moved up a little but that was it. The expression on her face remained blank, but Jack could tell she was working hard to hold it. She pretended to read the cover of the end book. There was not much written there but she took some time to finish.

'Yes,' she said, finally. 'Yes, I think I've heard of Edward Kass.' She looked up at Jack and gave him a smile. It was bright — and fake as a chocolate gold coin. 'Is he any good?'

'Not really.'

'They're sold, you say?'

'Just waiting to be delivered.'

'What a pity.' She straightened up. 'I remember now. He was actually one of the poets recommended to me.'

'Really?'

'No chance then?'

'I don't think so.' Jack picked up one of the books and flipped through the pages. 'My collector wouldn't appreciate it. I mean, what if I were holding the books for you and—'

'I'm happy to pay a little more,' she interrupted. 'Would that persuade you?'

Jack leaned back against the counter, shaking his head. 'Look,' he said, in a stiff voice, 'I've got a dinner date tonight and I'd like to spend too much time getting ready for it. I'm going to need more than the offer of a few extra dollars to stay open.'

The woman looked at him, surprised. Jack could see her thoughts flit over her eyes, like a line of fast cars reflecting past dark windows. She was having trouble keeping up with them.

'Is your collector a man by the name of Hammond Kasprowicz?' There was more than a little venom in her voice.

'You tell me.'

She walked off. At the front door she stopped and turned around. 'I don't know exactly what to say to you,' she said, huffed and puffed now, like she had received bad service at the bank. 'But you shouldn't sell those books to Hammond Kasprowicz.'

'And why's that?'

'Because he's a complete and utter bastard, that's why.'

The pale skin of her neck broke out in angry blotches. It was obvious she was a woman who did not indulge her temper often. She tugged at the bag on her shoulder.

'Aren't bastards allowed to own books?' asked Jack.

'Not that bastard. And not those books.'

'You still haven't told me —'

'Oh, shut up!' she yelled. It was loud and sudden. 'He's burning them. Is that good enough?' She covered her face with one of her long woolly sleeves and started to sob. Through the tears and the thick, rib-knitted wool she cried: 'He's burning my father's books!'

~7~

JACK BROUGHT A CHAIR OUT from behind the counter and offered it to the woman. She sat down and blew her nose into a bright yellow handkerchief.

'Would you like a drink of water?'

'No, thank you, I'm fine.' She dabbed at her eyes. 'Please forgive me.'

Jack smiled, a quick friendly smile, like he sometimes gave babies on the bus.

'I'm Celia Mitten.'

'Jack Susko.'

She slipped the bag from her shoulder and lowered it to the floor. Under the blue-tinged fluorescent light her face looked weary and Jack had an idea that Celia Mitten did not always feel as colourful as her clothing.

'I live with my father in Potts Point,' she said. 'He's old now, not very well. For the last twenty years he's been trying to complete his final collection. His masterpiece. He still writes every day, from eight in the morning until noon. In the kitchen. It's been quite stressful lately, because he's not well.' She looked into her lap, picked something off her skirt. 'He believes he'll die before he completes his work.'

Jack imagined Kass in the kitchen. Eight until noon must have been a barrel of laughs in there. The poet and his burning brain.

'If he knew what Hammond Kasprowicz was doing,' said Celia, shaking her head. 'My God ...' Her neck flushed again.

Jack put his hands in his coat pockets. 'How do you know Hammond Kasprowicz is burning his books?'

'Because he sent them to us, that's how. A box of ashes in the mail. Luckily I was there when it arrived. Here'—she reached down into her bag—'you can read the note yourself.'

She found the note and held it up. 'It's typed,' she said. Then, defensively: 'There's no name. But I know it's Hammond Kasprowicz.'

Jack took the small, cream envelope from her. *To Mr Edward Kass* was typed on the front. The letters were faded, punched through a ribbon that needed changing. Who used typewriters anymore? Jack slipped out the note. The paper was thick and grainy, the same colour as the envelope, and folded in half.

Soon it will be as if you never wrote anything at all.

'Sick, isn't it?' said Celia.

No name, no signature. Jack read the note a couple more times. Would Kasprowicz have written it? It seemed a little indirect. Or a touch too poetic.

'Does your father have any —'

'Enemies?' interrupted Celia. 'No. Apart from Hammond Kasprowicz.'

'Other poets?'

'I know what you're thinking. Petty jealousies and warring factions, all that. The battle for grants and prizes. I know all about it.' She adjusted her cardigan. 'But this? Burning another poet's books? Some of them can be vindictive, Mr Susko, and believe me, they have been. But not to this degree.'

'Have you confronted Kasprowicz about it?'

Celia laughed. 'Why? As if he would ever admit it.' Then she shook her head in disappointment and looked up at the ceiling. 'And just when there's interest in Dad's work again.'

'What do you mean?'

'People have been calling lately, wanting to speak to my father about his poetry. And there have been some enquiries about buying his archive as well.'

'Who wanted to buy his archive?'

'There were three or four calls, I can't remember exactly who now. University libraries, private collections, that sort of thing.'

Jack frowned, thinking.

Celia looked at him sadly. 'Please don't sell those books to Hammond Kasprowicz.'

'They're already paid for.'

'Haven't you been listening?'

'It's a big call, Ms Mitten. I'd like to hear what Hammond Kasprowicz had to say about it all.'

Celia stood up. Her chair scraped over the floor. She picked up her bag and pulled out a large red purse. She unclipped it and handed Jack a card.

Celia's Crystal Palace
Bridal Accessories
10b Macleay Street, Potts Point
tel. 93314411 fax. 93314423
email: celias@hotnet.com

'After you realise what kind of man Hammond Kasprowicz is,' she said stiffly, 'please call me.' She put the purse back into her bag. She looked around the bookshelves and then at Jack. 'I assume you must have some regard for the written word.'

'Sure,' he replied. 'When I can sell it.'

'Well, if it's just about the money —'

Jack held up his hand. 'No need to be rude, Ms Mitten. All you've given me so far is a story. It's not a bad story. In fact, it's pretty good. But I'm sure Hammond Kasprowicz could give me one, too.'

'Are you saying that I've made all this up?'

'I'm saying family sagas have a tendency towards melodrama.'

Jack watched her neck warm up again, a patchy blue-red like blackberry juice. An old girlfriend once told him that it was a sign of energy blocked in the throat: not saying what you wanted to say. Jack's ex had been interested in stuff like that.

'My father is at home, Mr Susko, quite ill and depressed,' said Celia Mitten firmly. 'I have a package of his burnt books hidden under the laundry sink. You are more than welcome to come by and see for yourself. I would be happy to offer you some afternoon tea for your trouble.'

~8~

JACK DECIDED ON HIS PALE GREY SUIT with the stovepipe pants. A dark plum shirt, black leather shoes and a splash of cologne. Lois moaned the whole time he was getting ready. He pushed her through the back door and put a bowl of food on the ground. She looked at him like he was joking.

'Hey, what can I say? I'll try not to be late.'

The front gate was open. Jack walked through and along the driveway. Ten metres from the house, security lights came on and lit the front yard like a stadium. Next door a dog went berserk. Jack almost dropped the wine bottle in his hand. Obviously he did not possess the nerves required for burglary. Another career option off the list. He climbed the front steps, crossed the verandah, and knocked. A few moments later, the front door opened.

'You must be Jack,' said a dark-haired woman with a hand on her hip. She was tall, and she was not wearing heels. 'Hi, I'm Sabine.'

Jack smiled. 'Nice to meet you, Sabine.'

She had an open, friendly face, its only blemish a pale scar about two centimetres long on the side of her chin. No doubt it was why she was wearing a little too much make-up for somebody dressed for exercise. Her hair was tied in a ponytail that had begun to come loose, and she wore a tight red tracksuit. She shook Jack's hand. There was a rock on her ring finger about the size of an avocado pip.

'Come in.'

Jack followed her down the hall. Sabine was full-bodied, looked old enough to have had a teenager or two, but possessed the sass of a younger woman in her walk.

'We were late getting back from the gym,' she said over her shoulder. 'Poor Anna's all last-minute rush, I'm afraid.'

She turned left into another hallway and led Jack into the kitchen. It was a large, airy room with an island bench, stainless steel appliances, and varnished timber cupboards over two walls. There were cream granite benches; the floor was of oversized terracotta tiles. A large, watercolour still life hung on the far wall: a bowl of bruised fruit, some vegetables, and a dead bird. Through some glass doors to his left, Jack noticed a paved patio area outside, half-lit by a spotlight attached to a corner of the house.

Sabine picked up a bottle. 'She's probably just fixing her hair. Glass of wine?'

'Cheers.' Jack put his own bottle down.

She poured a generous amount and passed it to him. Then she held up a small white bowl. 'You have to try these olives. They're fabulous. Do you like olives?'

Jack nodded, picked one out.

'I love them.' She popped a juicy kalamata into her mouth. Her lips were full and fleshy and slightly unbelievable. Her eyes were a rich brown and shone like billiard balls under lights. She rested a hip against the bench and looked Jack over. She chewed the olive and thought about what she saw. Jack sipped his wine and glanced around like he was interested in kitchen design.

Sabine dropped the pip into an ashtray. 'That's a lovely suit,' she said. 'Ermenegildo Zegna?'

'Is that the little Italian guy in Leichhardt?'

'Sorry?' she replied. Then she smiled, shook her head. 'Oh, yes. Anna said you were a smart-arse.'

'Nice to know she's been talking about me.'

'Not really. She won't tell me anything.' Sabine picked up another olive. 'Must be serious.'

It was hot in the kitchen. Above the stove an extraction fan made a lot of noise but did very little else.

'So, you work for Hammond then?'

'Not really.'

'Oh?'

'I'm doing a small job for him.'

'And you're a book dealer or something?'

'Purveyor of fine quality literature not necessarily in immaculate condition.'

'Nice living?'

'Will be. When my rich aunt dies.'

Sabine laughed. 'Why do it then?'

'I get to meet interesting people.'

'Like Hammond Kasprowicz? He's not that interesting.'

'Really?' Jack tried to read her face. Whatever was there was written in lemon juice.

She drank her wine, leaving a faint red stain of lips on the rim. 'You know you can't believe a word he says, don't you? Believe me, I know. I learned the hard way.' She brought the glass to her mouth again and paused. 'I used to fuck him.'

'I see.'

'Well, it was a while ago now. He wasn't quite so old then.' She laughed and drank more wine. 'Neither was I.'

Annabelle Kasprowicz walked into the kitchen. 'Have you kept an eye on my risotto?' she said to Sabine, shaking her head.

'We've already eaten it.'

'That'd be right.' Annabelle turned to Jack, smiling. 'Hello there.'

'Ms Kasprowicz,' he replied, thickly, like his mouth was suddenly full of honey. Annabelle kissed the air near his cheek. A butterfly the size of the *Times Comprehensive Atlas* woke up in his stomach and started flapping its wings.

'Are you well?' she asked.

'Very, thank you.'

'Good.' She reached up and adjusted her hair. It was still wet, done up in a loose chignon. Her skin was vaguely pink from a hot shower and glowed with the best moisturisers money could buy. Garnet drop earrings matched her lipstick.

'Sorry I'm late,' she said, nodding towards the stove as

she reattached a hair clip. 'The whole day's been one step ahead of me.'

'Don't worry about it. I had a hamburger on the way.'

Annabelle turned to Sabine. 'See what I mean?'

'Saw it before he opened his mouth.' Sabine picked up the bottle of wine and held it out. 'Top up?'

Jack brought his glass over.

'Is it me or is it hot in here?' asked Sabine.

As she poured the wine, Jack noticed that Annabelle was barefoot, her toenails the same shade of red as her earrings and lipstick. They were nice toes. She wore an oyster satin crossover top and a pair of jeans. A gold necklace disappeared down her front. Every inch of her was doing what she wanted it to do. She probably never had to ask.

'I didn't bother to check if you were vegetarian,' she said, lifting the lid on a pot on the stove.

'Vegan,' said Jack. 'I only eat organic tofu that has been humanely slaughtered.'

Sabine laughed heartily. She was definitely all carnivore.

Annabelle stirred the pot and replaced the lid. She began to set a sleek-looking, brushed metal, glass-top table.

'I thought we could eat in here. The dining room's too big and cold.' She pointed to a chair. 'Take a seat.'

Jack took his jacket off and hung it on the chair. He sat down and tried to look cool. As Annabelle went back and forth, he noticed small roses embroidered on the back pockets of her jeans.

Sabine sipped her wine. 'Jack was just saying that he thinks your father's interesting.'

'That's one way of describing him.'

'I've always liked *prick*,' said Sabine. 'And *bastard*. Oh, and I love *son of a bitch*.'

'Let's not get carried away in front of company now.'

'Then I would have said *motherfucker*.'

'You can take the girl out of the suburbs ...' Annabelle shook her head.

Sabine put a hand to her breast. 'I haven't offended you, have I, Jack?'

He grinned. Sabine had the sadist about her, no doubt. Jack bet she took her time with everything. Especially getting even. 'Of course not.'

Annabelle laid cutlery. 'Nobody forced you to marry him,' she said to Sabine, who was now looking at her reflection in the oven door, fixing her hair and readjusting her clothing. 'I still don't know why you did.'

Sabine swung around. 'Love, of course!'

'Oh, of course. What else?'

'You're such a bitch.' Sabine picked up a handbag from the floor and blew out a weary breath. 'All right then, honey. I'm off. Leave you to your *romance*.'

'Bye, baby.' Annabelle held Sabine's hands and kissed her on the lips. 'See you on Saturday.'

'Ten o'clock, Mario's, don't make me wait.'

Jack stood up. Sabine minced over and put her hand on his arm. She kissed him on both cheeks. 'Lovely to meet you, Jack. I'm sure I'll see you again.'

She walked out of the kitchen. 'Bye now,' she called back. 'Enjoy breakfast!' The front door banged shut.

Annabelle began to dish out the risotto. 'It's bone marrow and sage.' She smiled as she served him.

Jack lost a little feeling in his knees, like somebody was

blowing bubbles down there with a straw. 'So that's your ex-stepmother?'

Annabelle returned the pot of risotto to the stove. 'I'd hardly call her that. I didn't even know her when she was married to my father. I was away at boarding school that year. By the time I got back, it was over.' She began to dress a salad in a large glass bowl with frosted bunches of grapes engraved over it.

'You didn't meet her?'

'Oh, yes, a few times, but I didn't take any notice. She was one of many women my father paraded after my mother died. I got to know her later. After my father nearly killed her in a car accident.'

Jack remembered the scar on Sabine's chin. 'Nice they're still friends,' he said.

Annabelle sucked oil from her little finger. 'Sabine's main aim in life is to piss my father off as much as is humanly possible.'

'He doesn't mind you being friends?'

'No, he minds. That's why Sabine and I get on so well. We have a dislike of my father in common.'

She brought the salad over to the table and sat down. She picked up her glass of wine. 'Right then. Cheers.'

'Cheers.'

'I'm starving.'

Jack sipped his wine and then tried the risotto. There was a wholesomeness to the food, a warmth to the atmosphere in the kitchen. He had not expected it.

He stole glimpses of Annabelle as they ate. He could smell the warm soap freshness of her shower. 'That's the second relative of yours I've met today,' he said.

'Really? Who was the first?'

'Celia Mitten.'

The name floated between them for a moment, like the steam from the risotto. Annabelle looked down into her plate and teased the rice with her fork. 'What did Celia Mitten want?' She tried to sound casual, but it did not come out that way.

'She wanted me to stop selling the Edward Kass books to your father.'

'What?'

Jack picked up his glass. He regretted that he had brought it up. The wholesome atmosphere went up the extractor fan and blew out into the night. 'She thinks your father's burning Edward Kass's books.'

Annabelle put her fork down and wiped her mouth with a napkin. Jack had been expecting a more shocked expression. But then, what did he know? He supposed you could burn whatever the hell you wanted to burn when you were rich.

'Do you believe her?' Annabelle's voice was low, cautious.

'Should I?'

She paused. When she spoke again, her voice was clear and sharp and hot. 'Celia Mitten is a vindictive, hostile, evil bitch. I wouldn't believe what she said if it passed a lie-detector test.' She sounded pretty adamant.

'Why would she spin something like that then?'

Annabelle stood up. The cutlery on the table rattled. 'Have you got a cigarette?' she asked, impatiently. 'The risotto needs to cool down, it's too hot.'

'Sure.' Jack reached into his jacket hanging on the chair and took out his pack and a lighter.

Annabelle opened the glass doors onto the patio. Jack lit their cigarettes and they stood there and smoked. The air was cold as stainless steel.

Jack drew on his cigarette. He looked up into the night: the earlier clouds had cleared. It was a beautiful winter sky, fresh as a tarmac after rain.

'So what did she say exactly?'

'She said that Kasprowicz had sent her father a box full of ashes. His burnt books. The note implied there would be more to come. Maybe all of them.'

'She's lying. You don't know her. It's all about money.'

'What money?'

'The fucking money they didn't get! The inheritance!' A frown dug into her forehead. She closed her eyes and breathed deeply. When she opened them again, they were lustreless, resigned. 'It all went to my father. Celia's never let it go. Never will.' She dropped her cigarette and stepped on it.

'But why would she accuse—'

'I don't know! Why would I know?'

She chewed her bottom lip. Jack wished he could apply for the job. For some reason there was now only thirty centimetres between them. And closing? Maybe it was the alignment of the stars. He flicked his cigarette away behind him.

Annabelle looked up into his eyes. Tension slipped from her face. Her features softened. 'You've got no idea what I've been through with this family,' she said, her voice sounding sorry for her, if nobody else was. 'No idea at all.'

'Maybe you should tell me about it.'

'Maybe I should.'

'I'm a good listener.'

'So why don't you shut up.'

Two seconds later, Annabelle Kasprowicz had her arms around him. Jack watched her lips travel towards him in slow motion through time and space, slightly open, promising death by softness. He held her to him and obliged with an opposite and equal reaction. They kissed. Jack stopped thinking. All was well in the world.

Sometimes a minute can be a long time. You can even forget where you are in one good, long minute. Then a voice from the kitchen reminded Jack exactly where he was.

'Hi Mum.'

Annabelle pushed herself away from Jack as though he had caught fire.

'Louisa, what are you doing home?' She stepped back into the kitchen. Her daughter stared at Jack. If there had been a cigarette in his mouth, her eyes would have lit it. His eyebrows might have gone up, too.

'Nina got upset with her mother and took off.'

'Who brought you over?'

'I called Dad. He's in the car. We're going out for food.'

Annabelle glanced at Jack. 'Louisa was at a wedding rehearsal. She's a bridesmaid for her cousin.'

Jack nodded. He was imagining himself punching Durst through his car window. He walked back into the kitchen, closing the patio door behind him.

'I remember you,' said Louisa. She tilted her head to the right, the stern look was replaced with a smirk. 'You're the gas man.'

'The best in the business.'

'He's cute, Mum. Nice shoulders.'

'Don't be smart.'

Louisa crossed her arms. 'When are you going to introduce him to Dad?'

'We've already met,' said Jack. He was glad he was no longer a nineteen-year-old, hormones surging, confused, loud, fragile. Girls like Louisa had always eaten poor bastards like that for breakfast.

'Oh, good. Then you can say hello.' She smiled at Jack, then winked at her mother.

'That's enough, Louisa.'

'I'll just go get him.' She walked out of the kitchen and down the hall.

'You might have to set another place,' said Jack, bristling.

'This isn't funny.' Annabelle walked over and picked up her glass from the dining table and drank: but wine was the wrong drink. It was not for going down quickly. She coughed. 'She won't bring him in.'

'Maybe he's hungry.'

'She won't bring him in.'

The extraction fan whined. Jack strained his ears, listening for the front door, for footsteps down the hall. Annabelle was listening, too. A minute later, they both heard them.

Here he comes. Jack dropped his right hand to his side and flexed his fingers. His heart beat hard in his chest. He had never thumped a middle-aged metrosexual before.

~9~

HAMMOND KASPROWICZ WAS FAR FROM MARXIST, but he strode into the kitchen like a politburo minister of the former Union of Soviet Socialist Republics. His face was flushed and sweaty: under the whiteness of his hair, his colour reminded Jack of a hot saveloy. He was dressed in a charcoal grey suit, white shirt, and a broad, pale yellow tie. There was a black leather briefcase in his hand. He dropped it onto the floor beside the island bench and immediately began tugging at the Windsor knot around his neck.

'You should teach your daughter some manners.'

He said it without looking at Annabelle at all. His voice was gruff, but tired. He removed his jacket, then checked the pockets before throwing it onto a stool.

Annabelle walked over to the dinner table and sat down. Jack stood looking at Kasprowicz, wondering when the old man was going to acknowledge his presence.

'I thought you were flying back tomorrow night,' said Annabelle.

Kasprowicz grunted. 'Obviously.' He opened a cupboard door and removed a bottle of Scotch. 'Are you well, Mr Susko?'

'Any better I'd burst. Yourself?'

No reply. Kasprowicz hunched his broad, round back over the bottle and cracked the cap.

'Sit down, Jack.' Annabelle motioned to his chair.

'Yes.' Kasprowicz poured himself three fat fingers of Scotch. 'Please, don't let me disturb your dinner.' He held onto the edge of the granite bench-top, tilted his head back and threw half the Scotch down his throat.

'You're a smooth operator, Susko,' he said, his back still to them. 'One minute you're knee-deep in smelly old books, the next you're in my kitchen, enjoying a meal with my daughter.' He brought the glass up to his mouth again. 'I can only hope you've applied yourself as tenaciously to my little job.'

Jack grinned. Kasprowicz was quick: he might be old, but his brain ticked over like it had been engineered in Stuttgart. 'I'm giving it my full attention, Hammond. I didn't know you were such a fan of your brother's work.'

Hammond Kasprowicz turned around. 'So you know.' He sipped his drink and glanced at his daughter. She had her back to him but shifted in her seat under his gaze. 'That's almost impressive. Maybe I'll have to find more jobs for you.' He rubbed his chin and pulled at his tie some more.

'Though I worry about your confidentiality.'

Jack smiled. He could have cut the nonchalance with a chainsaw. 'I worry about your disclosure,' he replied.

Glass in hand, Kasprowicz picked his briefcase up from the floor. 'Some things just aren't your business, Mr Susko. You have your job and you've been paid.' Kasprowicz rolled his shoulders. 'When can I expect a delivery? Have you had much success?'

'Moderate. But competition doesn't help.'

Kasprowicz's brows angled down and shadowed his eyes like furry awnings. He seemed genuinely surprised. 'Competition?'

Jack nodded. 'That's right.'

Kasprowicz stared thoughtfully at his glass of Scotch. Jack waited, watching him.

Annabelle broke the silence 'Why are you after Edward's books?'

Kasprowicz frowned like a High Court judge. 'And why would that be any of your concern?'

'Not so much my concern,' said Annabelle. 'Rather Celia Mitten's.'

'What are you talking about?'

Annabelle turned to look at her father. Kasprowicz pushed his chin out.

'Are you burning Edward's books?' she said, a little stronger than matter-of-factly. 'Is that why you've got Jack searching for them? So that you can burn them, put the ashes in a box and send them to a sick old man?'

Kasprowicz shook his head, disappointed and annoyed, as though Annabelle had just told him she was pregnant by the gardener. 'You've been drinking,' he said. The man was a Fourth-Dan Black Belt in the delivery of contempt. 'Who told you this nonsense?'

Annabelle stood up, determined. She knew she had already gone too far. Even the pot plants knew it. 'Are you burning Edward's books?' she repeated.

'You might want to lose the tone.'

'Then why else would you want them?'

Hammond Kasprowicz looked at Jack and then back at his daughter. His face was as hard as the bust of a Roman emperor. He did not care that the risotto was getting cold. 'It's not your business,' he said. That was it. Question time was over. He picked up his jacket, turned and walked out of the kitchen. His footsteps were loud but unhurried down the hall.

For a few moments, neither of them spoke. Annabelle went over to the stove and switched the extraction fan off. Jack drank some wine. His stomach mumbled something nasty about being empty.

'Not much of a dinner,' said Annabelle.

'It's still here.'

'I'm sorry. And it was meant to be an apology.'

Jack stood up, slowly. Obviously time to go. 'Nothing to be sorry about.'

'I'll call you. Maybe we could try this again. In a restaurant.'

'Any time.'

Jack slipped on his coat, adjusted the sleeves and collar of his shirt. Annabelle crossed her arms over her chest. There was going to be no goodnight kiss.

'Do you think he burnt them?'

'You know your father better than I do.'

'Nobody knows my father.'

She stared at the terracotta tiles. Jack walked towards the hallway door. She did not look up when he said goodbye. He stepped quietly out of the kitchen and made his way to the front door.

Outside, he lit a cigarette, walked to the gate and glanced back at the house. It looked cold and empty, even though he knew there were people inside.

Jack changed his mind about going home. He was hungry. He stopped in Paddington, ordered a pizza and bought a bottle of wine. Then he hailed another taxi and directed it into the city.

It was still quite early. Lois was no doubt curled up somewhere in a neighbour's apartment, not thinking about him at all. Sometimes home could feel a little empty, especially on wet Monday nights. Jack wanted the dusty silence of Susko Books, and some Charles Mingus on the stereo for company. Tonight, maybe *At the Bohemia, 1955.* And then ease into that long bottle of red. Pick out some books, open the pages at random and see what he gets. The outside world where it should be — outside.

He had kissed her. Thirty sweet seconds. Hardly enough to count for a memory.

'Just here's fine, thanks.' Jack held the pizza box off his lap and paid the cab driver. The smell had filled the taxi, greasing the stale air inside.

A street-sweeper swished loudly around the corner and Jack stepped back from the kerb as it drove past. The sky was still clear, the stars in crisp focus. It was cold, but no rain tonight. Just ahead, Queen Victoria sat in her usual spot, spilling abundantly out of her chair, the weight of the Empire in her sagging bronze jowls.

York Street. Somebody sat on the top steps to Susko Books, talking on a mobile phone, his back to the street. Jack crossed over. He watched the young guy stand up and pocket his mobile phone. Then just as he walked up, Jack caught a flash of light that seemed to come from the front door of his shop. Surprised, he stopped at the top of the steps and waited a moment, trying to see through the shadowed glass. Nothing. Then as he took a step down, the light flashed again and darted about in the darkness. What the hell?

Jack quickly put the pizza and bottle of wine down and called out to the phone guy just walking away. 'Hey! You! Call the cops. Somebody's in my shop!'

The guy turned around. He was a young man in his twenties, wearing green camouflage pants, a beanie and a thick, hooded windcheater. 'What?' He gave Jack a wary, petulant look.

'Someone's broken into my fucking shop. Could you call the cops?'

The young man's eye's widened. 'Yeah, sure man, no worries.' He reached for his phone and flipped it open.

'Tell them it's Susko Books, on York Street. The guy's still in there.'

Jack sprinted around into Market Row. The lane was empty. He slowed down as he approached the rear door to his bookshop. The sound of traffic carried down from George Street but seemed a long way off.

He pulled the keys out of his pocket. As he neared the rear door, he saw they would not be necessary: somebody had taken out the lock and handle with a sledgehammer.

Jack held his breath and pushed the door slowly: it started to creak so he held it fast. It was open just enough for him to slip through. But wait there or go inside? He was unsure. He needed a weapon.

His heart thumped. He stepped inside. Jack Susko had never held a gun in his life, but he was sure it would have felt better than the old, 1970s *Smoker's Please* ashtray he picked up off the floor behind the door. First thing tomorrow he was buying an aluminium baseball bat.

There were noises up ahead, somewhere near the counter: shuffling of papers, drawers being opened, books dropped to the floor, a chair shoved aside. An old coffee mug full of pens spilled and a second later smashed on the floor. The intruder swore. Then the dull drum echo of Jack's small, wastepaper bin as a palm hit the side a couple of times and emptied it.

Jack edged forwards. He held the ashtray in his right hand, ready to swing. It was dark but he knew where the shelves were, knew which way to go. Every now and then the intruder's torchlight reflected off something in the shop, a quick flash of glass, of metal, a sudden grainy patch of ceiling or wall, then gone. It was like being underwater at night.

For a moment, complete silence. Jack stopped. Then he heard paper being torn. Followed by the scrape and scratch of a lighter flicking sparks. He took another step. The ashtray he was carrying banged against the metal corner of a bookshelf. He froze. Three seconds later, a beam of thin, harsh light caught him full in the face.

Things happened pretty quickly after that.

~10~

THE TORCH SNAPPED OFF and somebody started running. Jack stood where he was, trying to focus on what was ahead of him, blinking away the brightness. As he did, something like a ten-pin bowling ball struck him in the stomach at about sixty kilometres an hour. Jack doubled over, groaning.

Whoever had head-butted him tried to shove Jack aside and scramble past, but the shelves were narrow there, between Classics, Religion and History. Blindly, Jack managed to grab hold of the flap of a jacket. He grimaced and pulled, letting his weight fall to the floor. The assailant remained on his feet but Jack forced him to bend over. The man writhed and flayed. Jack held on. He tried to curl an arm around the man's legs and trip him up. Elbows and fists rained down, mainly catching Jack in the arm and shoulder, but a couple stung the side of his head. Then Jack remembered his suit and felt a surge of anger. He pulled harder on the jacket and as he did so lifted himself up a little off the floor. His head came up above the level of his hands. Just high enough for the guy to get a good look at it.

A terrific pain burst in the middle of Jack's face: his nose exploded like a ripe tomato. Wet warmth began to spread around the general area. He let go of the jacket, collapsed to the floor, and put his hands to his face.

'Stupid fucker,' barked a thin, angry voice.

Jack was grabbed by the lapels of his jacket. He blinked and looked up. A dark face was bent over him: he could just see the whites of the man's eyes, glazed blue-grey in the weak light of the street lamps outside.

'Should've stayed at home, eh?'

Jack tried to breathe, but his nose was full of hot gravel.

The man pushed Jack away and straightened up. He reached into his coat pocket and pulled out a knife.

Jack caught a glimpse of the blade, liquid silver like the flash of a fish in murky water. 'Oh, shit!' He tried to get to his feet. Another punch to the head stopped him, though he managed to slip the force of the blow away from his face with his arm.

'Should've stayed at home—'

The back door to Susko Books swung open and banged against the wall. A corridor of muted, night-time city light spread down the aisle of books. The man with the knife turned and looked towards the rear of the shop. Jack squinted at the face of his attacker: it was the son of a bitch who had tried to sell him the stolen books earlier that day.

'You there?' called out the guy with the mobile from the street. His voice was frail and nervous. 'Hello?'

Jack filled his lungs and climbed to his feet. 'Over here!' The intruder swung around. His arm shot out. The knife blade reached out in a pointy curve. Jack back-pedalled but found a bookshelf. Frantic, he tried to push himself along the uneven spines. He did not get far.

An instant later, a hot stripe drew itself briefly across his stomach, just about where his appendix would have been if he still had it. The moment his hand went there, he could feel dampness seeping through his shirt. Jack Susko slipped down the bookcase to the floor again.

The assailant ran towards the back door. Somebody swore and then there were scuffling footsteps and a crash and then nothing. A few moments later the young guy from the street walked in, stepping cautiously through the shop.

Jack sat himself up and leaned against the bookshelf. 'There's a light switch just beside the door.'

'Shit, are you all right?' The guy ran over.

'I hope so. Did you get hold of the cops?'

'They're on their way.' He knelt down beside Jack. 'The fucker just rammed past me!' he said. Then he took a better look at Jack. 'Oh, shit!'

Jack pressed down where the knife had slashed him. 'Reckon you could grab the towel from behind the counter? Should be on a shelf there somewhere.'

'Yeah, sure, sure.'

Jack put his head back. He turned and let it hang over his left shoulder. The shop lights flickered on, fluorescent tubes popping with harsh blue light, and he closed his eyes from the glare. When he opened them, he noticed a book sticking out a little from the shelf, just there beside him. He turned his head a little more and read the spine: *After We Die, What Then?* by George W. Meek.

Nothing like a good sign at the end of a bad day.

'This is Detective Peterson,' said one of the police officers. 'He'll need to ask you a few more questions.'

Detective Geoff Peterson was a tall man in a plain navy-blue suit. He had a wide face, pale complexion and small, dry blue eyes set close together. The remains of acne scars dappled his cheeks. His close-cropped sandy hair was receding in a neat V from his forehead, and his ears stuck out from his head. They were fleshy, like oysters, and large enough to pick up FM radio signals. His hands were in his pockets and he stared down at the end of his plain, light blue tie, brooding. Absently, he scratched the back of his head. Then he rubbed his face like a man who could do with some sleep.

As Jack watched him, the detective lifted his head and looked straight at him. His eyes caught Jack square, like headlights flicked onto high beam. His face was set firm. And then he winked. Surprised, Jack looked away. What the hell was that about? Peterson kept his eyes on him for a moment longer and Jack felt them crawling over his face, scrutinising him. It was not a nice feeling.

A uniformed police officer waited beside the detective with a notepad. Jack sat uncomfortably in a chair that had been brought out from behind the counter. The ambulance officers had cleaned him up, stuck a cold pack on his face, and dressed the knife wound. It was not deep, but a few stitches up at St Vincent's Emergency ward were recommended. Jack had already answered questions and given a statement and was keen to get home, but now Detective Peterson was here and he wanted to go over a few things.

'Is this going to take much longer?' asked Jack, irritated. He had swallowed a couple of painkillers, but his head still felt like an egg in boiling water.

Peterson grinned, but the smile vanished before taking hold. 'So you arrived about what time?' he said, as though they were halfway through a conversation. He squinted at Jack like a schoolteacher who already knew the answer to the question.

'I don't know exactly.' Jack took the cold pack off his nose. 'Sometime between eight-thirty and nine, I suppose. Whatever time it was when the guy from the street called you. You should know when he rang.'

Peterson did not respond. He paced around a little. The uniformed police officer stood perfectly still and scribbled in his notebook.

'And you say nothing was taken?'

'I don't know yet. He smashed my pen mug, though.'

Peterson took one hand out of his pocket and stroked his tie, running a finger down it smoothly, like a cut-throat razor over a strap. 'I don't suppose there'd be much cash lying around here, would there?' he said, raising his eyebrows on the word *cash*. 'I mean, what's a second-hand book set you back. A dollar fifty? A couple of bucks? You'd have to sell a few to get a stash together.' He nodded, agreeing with himself. 'Take a while.'

Jack did not answer.

The detective stood up straighter, pushed his chin out a

little and carefully adjusted his tie. 'Do you have a safe?'

'No.'

'Cash box?'

Jack laughed and then grimaced because it hurt. 'Shoe box,' he said.

'Ah, I see. And how's trade been?' Peterson's tone was cool, conversational, but full of pins, like a cheap business shirt.

'Fine.' Jack noticed the uniformed officer had put his notebook away.

Peterson nodded. 'What days do you bank?'

'Whenever I get a hundred bucks together,' said Jack. 'Usually the autumn solstice.'

'That's pretty funny,' said Peterson. He did not laugh. His voice wore steel-capped boots and stepped all over Jack. He slipped his hands into his pockets again and leaned back against the counter.

Jack had to turn a little to keep his eyes on him. The slash across his stomach burnt.

'So what I want to know is why somebody would break into a second-hand bookshop in the first place?' The detective looked up at the ceiling as he spoke, as though he was thinking out loud. Then he looked at the police officer there beside him. 'I mean, really, what could you want? Obviously there's no money. Just old books.'

'Rare books?' said the officer, as if he had struggled to think of the answer.

Peterson flashed a grin and looked quickly at Jack. 'Doesn't look particularly *antique* in here though, does it?' He checked out his shoes and then brushed something off his pants. 'Any rare books, Mr Susko?' he said, still smiling. 'Anything worth more than half-a-dozen dollars in here?'

Jack shifted his weight onto his left buttock. His nose throbbed. 'Not today.'

'So why would our friend take the risk? If you're going to smash a door and have no qualms about pulling a knife, why not a jewellery store? A bottleshop or a newsagency? Even a café would give you a better return.'

Jack had started to dislike Detective Geoff Peterson about five minutes ago. The feeling was now taking root like a noxious weed. He put the cold pack down and reached over the counter for his cigarettes. He put one in his mouth and then struck a match against the box. Before lighting it, he paused. 'Maybe if you catch him,' he said, 'you could ask him.'

Peterson shot a look at Jack. If it had been a bullet, it might have grazed his ear.

Jack lit the cigarette and tossed the spent match onto the counter. He drew back and then exhaled slowly, watching the detective through the smoke.

'But I was wondering if *you* had any ideas, Mr Susko,' said Peterson, smoothly, flattery lining his voice like artificial sweetener. 'Think about it. There's nothing to steal, but he brings a knife and attacks you.' Peterson looked at the officer again. 'Makes you wonder, doesn't it?'

'About what?' said Jack. He was starting to feel like he needed a lawyer.

Peterson grinned. 'You say you recognised the man?'

Jack tapped ash into the palm of his hand. He could see where Peterson was going with his questions. It was starting to annoy him. 'Could you pass me the ashtray over there?' he said, pointing.

The uniformed police officer slid it across so that Jack

could reach. Jack brushed the ash from his palm into it and then smoothed the tip of his cigarette against the aluminium side of the ashtray. 'Yes, I've already told you. He was in earlier today.'

'And a week or so ago, too, you said?'

'I think so.'

'What for?' asked Peterson, sternly.

Jack kept his voice calm. 'He was trying to sell me stolen books.'

'Was this the first time or had you used him before?' Detective Peterson was getting a little nasty.

Jack closed his eyes and breathed deeply. He could feel the Panadeine Forte the ambulance guys had given him finally beginning to work. The day was catching up with him, lapping at his body in long, foamy waves. It was not an unpleasant sensation. 'He's my main supplier.'

'I wouldn't joke, Mr Susko.' Peterson took out his keys, looked at them and then slipped them back into his pocket. 'Do you owe anybody any money?' he said.

'Does that include my grandmother?'

Peterson smiled, like a croupier about to take all Jack's chips. 'Only if she's capable of sending a guy around with a knife.'

'Well, she always says I never come around. They can get crazy, old people.'

'We'll be in touch, Mr Susko.'

Jack looked over at the uniformed police officer. 'Can I grab a lift to the hospital?'

'Can't you drive yourself?'

'Not without a car.'

The police officer glanced at Peterson.

'You could always lend me one,' added Jack.

The detective frowned but nodded to the officer. 'Okay.'

'Oh, thanks ever so much,' replied Jack.

The officer walked off. Detective Peterson came over and stood beside Jack. He carefully buttoned the middle button of his coat. Without looking at Jack, he said: 'Susko. That's an interesting name. Be hard to forget.'

Jack drew on his cigarette and then tapped it into the ashtray. 'Cost me my job in espionage.'

'Kind of rings a bell for me.'

Jack looked up at Peterson and watched him pull at his tie a little, loosening it. He noticed a shaving rash just above the detective's collar. He hoped it had been irritating him all day.

'That'd be my uncle,' he said, deadpan. 'Harry Susko and the Sausage Boys. They were big in the seventies. Cabaret. They had a fantastic piano accordion player.'

'No, I don't reckon that's it.' Detective Peterson shook his head. 'It's right on the tip of my tongue. But I just can't remember. Susko. Susko.' He scratched his chin. 'I suppose it'll come to me later.'

Jack put a hand on the counter and slowly stood up. 'Hope it doesn't keep you up all night.'

Peterson rubbed his hands together. 'Goodnight, Mr Susko. Careful with that cut.'

The officers were finishing up. Jack walked gingerly behind the counter and looked into the rubbish bin. He glanced at the police and then carefully reached in. His copy of *Entropy House*. The bottom corner was lightly singed black from the bite of a flame. He brushed at it, then rubbed the greasy stain between his fingers. It smudged grey. He wondered if Hammond Kasprowicz would notice. Jack would be sure to point it out.

It was after 11.00 p.m. There were two other people in the waiting room at St Vincent's Hospital Emergency ward. A dark-haired twenty-something, dressed in a sweaty white T-shirt and faded jeans, sat passed out in one of the plastic chairs, star-fished, his limbs and head spilling awkwardly over the edges as though he had been shot. His friend—obviously still buzzing from whatever they had taken—nodded his head and drummed his knees and chewed gum beside him. Occasionally he leaned over to his comatose friend and said: 'You'll be right. Just breathe.'

Good advice.

Jack stared at the double doors that led into the surgery. Finally, they swung open. A nurse called out: 'Mr Susko?'

Jack followed her through. On the other side he found a few more people sitting around, waiting: some blank-faced, some worried, a couple asleep. He wondered if Monday nights were always like this. A handful of hospital staff milled around the narrow hall and walked in and out of doors. An orderly wheeled a machine down the corridor. A middle-aged woman in a pale blue uniform was refilling a water dispenser with plastic cups, while another mopped the area around it. And a little further down, Celia Mitten sat on a chair, flipping through a magazine.

The nurse told Jack to wait. He nodded and remained on his feet. As the nurse disappeared into a cubicle, he walked down towards Celia Mitten.

'Hello.'

Celia looked up and swallowed a quick gulp of air. 'My God, what are you doing here?'

'Gang fight. What about you?'

She glanced behind her through an open door. The bed in the room was unoccupied. 'It's my father. He's had a turn. I think it was a heart attack.'

'Is he okay?'

Tears rose in her eyes. Jack noticed she was wearing the same clothes as when he had seen her earlier that day.

'I don't know,' she said, a little breathless. 'They've taken him somewhere for tests.'

Jack saw a nurse coming towards him. Celia blew her nose into a crumpled tissue that she pulled out of her sleeve.

'Another package arrived with a note,' she said, trying to swallow her sobs. 'I was with you when it arrived.'

Jack winced as he shifted his weight from one leg to the other. 'What did the note say?'

Celia did not answer. The nurse had stopped beside them.

'This way, Mr Susko.'

Jack smiled at the nurse and then turned to Celia. 'Wait for me, I won't be long. Okay?' He patted her gently on the arm.

Celia Mitten nodded, wiping under her eyes with the tissue.

Jack was ushered into an examination cubicle. He sat down in a plastic fold-out chair. He could hear groaning next door and the odd squeak of rubber shoes, then an orderly telling somebody to take a deep breath. He lifted the corner of his shirt and looked down at the bandage on his stomach: blood had soaked through.

'Mr Susko? I'm Doctor Armstrong.' The doctor walked in. She dragged the cubicle curtains together with two swift movements. 'After some stitches, I believe?'

She was young looking, maybe mid-thirties, and had sandy hair tied in a plait. Her eyebrows were darker, curved over large brown eyes that glistened in the stark, tiled room, lit by nauseating fluorescent light. A kind, soft face. She was slim, athletically curved, dressed in grey slacks, a white short-sleeve shirt and a pair of red Adidas sneakers.

'Shirt off and flat on the bed, thanks.'

'Oh, good. I was hoping you'd do all the work.'

The doctor smiled but continued with her preparations. 'Do you want this to hurt, Mr Susko?'

'Whatever you're into, Doc. Just hit me with some pethidine and go for it.'

Jack removed his jacket and shirt and lay down on a narrow bed. The plastic sheet beneath him popped thickly like bubble wrap. The doctor wheeled over a tray of bandages and bottles and long pointy instruments. Jack closed his eyes. He had never been good with this kind of thing.

It did not take long. He received a tetanus injection as well, which only added to his wooziness. He thanked the doctor, who handed him a strip of painkillers.

'One every three hours. Better if you can go longer, though. They're strong.'

Jack moved out of the examination cubicle and walked down to where Celia had been. She was gone. When he asked at the front desk, they told him that she had already left with her father.

'Heart attack?'

The male nurse scoffed. 'Panic attack.'

~11~

IT WAS WELL AFTER 10.00 A.M. the next morning before Jack climbed carefully out of bed. As tired as he was when he got home, he had spent most of the night waking up every five minutes. Each time he moved, something hurt. He had to breathe through his mouth. And all his half-dreams were surreal and unsettling, playing out the last week of his life like a Buñuel montage. Detective Peterson had haunted most of them.

He dragged on a white bathrobe and pulled open the curtains. He rubbed his eyes at the day. Mid-morning light sharpened itself on the wet glass of the window. The damp grey wall opposite looked as lonely as it did yesterday. His nose ached. He needed a cigarette and a strong cup of coffee.

Before Jack had crossed the lounge-room floor he heard Lois outside the front door, complaining. When he let her in she looked up, held his eyes for a moment, and then sauntered into the flat, offering only a quick, unimpressed miaow in greeting.

'Nice to see you, too.'

He followed her into the kitchen. She nudged up against Jack's shins and flicked her tail. He bent down and gave her a scratch behind the ear. 'How about you go into work for me today, huh?'

He was in no hurry to get to Susko Books. The police had barred the damaged rear door from the inside, so for the time being nobody was going to get in. He had earned at least half a day off. And there was no boss to convince. Just a pity the sick day had to come out of his own pocket.

He opened his bathrobe and inspected the bandage on his stomach. Blood-tinged yellow fluid had seeped through the dressing. The whole area was sore to the touch. Lucky Doctor Armstrong had given him the good stuff. He wondered which clothes he was going to be able to wear.

Jack flicked the kettle on. He spooned some coffee into a plunger and then lit a cigarette. While the water boiled, he dialled Hammond Kasprowicz's mobile number.

'Yes?'

'Hammond, how are you?'

'Who is this?'

'Jack Susko. Your employee of the month.'

There was a slight hesitation. Then, firmly: 'Yes?'

'Why am I searching for your brother's books?'

'Are you on drugs, Susko?'

'Why would someone want to burn them?'

'Listen here, I'm not going to —'

'Hey!' Jack shouted into the phone. Lois bolted into the lounge room. 'I want you to listen very carefully.' Jack was pacing around his tiny kitchen now. 'Otherwise the next call you get'll be the cops. Clear?'

Silence. Then: 'Don't threaten me, boy.'

'Don't call me boy, grandpa. What d'you want with your brother's books?'

Kasprowicz sighed, as he might at an annoying child. 'I don't see what business it is of yours.' His voice was cool and precise. 'Would you mind telling me what this is all about?'

Jack controlled himself. 'Sure, I'll tell you. Somebody broke into my shop last night, smashed a couple of things and then poked my guts with a knife. Just in case I needed to let off a little digestive gas. How's that sound?'

Kasprowicz cleared his throat. 'I'm sorry if —'

'Hold the concern, Hammond. I wouldn't believe you anyway.' Jack dragged on the cigarette. 'Just before the knife said hello to my belly button, he tried to smoke up a couple of books in my rubbish bin. Poetry books, Hammond, by a certain Edward Kass. What do you think that's all about?'

'How would I know?' Kasprowicz turned on his growling-bear tone again.

Jack grinned, running his fingers through his hair. 'Okay,' he said, his voice calm, resigned. 'You can either tell me what the fuck's going on, or, if you prefer, I'll let Detective Peterson know exactly what the guy was doing and how it's connected with you. And because it's the cops, I'll be sure to mention that the books he was trying to burn in my rubbish bin are the same books somebody is sending to your estranged brother, the morbid poet of Potts Point, also burnt and with nasty little messages attached to the parcels. Should I go on? Because I can.'

'That won't be necessary. Just a moment.'

Jack waited. He heard voices, disjointed words down the line.

Then Kasprowicz coughed and said: 'This afternoon is impossible, I'm extremely busy. But I can give you twenty minutes tomorrow. At the house. One o'clock.'

'What's wrong with right now?'

'I'm a busy man, Mr Susko, or didn't you hear me? And I'd prefer not to discuss the matter over the phone.'

Kasprowicz's voice sounded genuine.

Jack relented. 'One o'clock.'

He went into the lounge room to select some music. Something bluesy and dark. Something mean. Something by the Stones, he decided. As Lois looked up from in front of the heater, the opening riffs of 'Midnight Rambler' strutted out of the speakers, smoky and round and full of intent. Lois yawned, flashing her sharp little fangs. Jack sat back in the Eames chair and put his feet on the coffee table. He smoked his cigarette. It was time for him to sharpen his fangs a little, too.

The scene of the crime: a drawer pulled out and emptied on the floor; shattered wineglass, busted mug, spilled pens and pencils; a few books tossed about, papers too, all content to stay where they lay. A stapler knocked from the counter was splayed like a broken jaw. Jack surveyed the damage and felt surprisingly calm. He walked slowly around the bookshelves: no other disruptions. The back door looked okay in the dim light and from a distance, but worse as he got closer. He frowned, bothered by the impending hassle and expense of getting it replaced.

He returned to his desk and picked up the phone. The dial tone told him a message was waiting. Chester Sinclair's smarmy voice came through. Jack hung his head as he listened.

Mr Susko, taking another day off? Tsk tsk, you'll be in the bankruptcy courts if you're not careful. Small business requires dedication and long hours. Lucky for you, you've got me. How does a dozen Edward Kass books sound? Like money, maybe? Give me a call.

Jack hung up the phone, keeping his hand on the receiver. Fucking Chester Sinclair. But even as he shook his head in exasperation, Jack began flipping through the address book with his free hand. He picked up the phone again and dialled the number for Jack and the Bookstalk.

He tapped a pen impatiently against the counter. He wondered where the hell Sinclair had found a dozen Edward Kass books. The phone rang a few times before being answered.

'Hello, Bookstalk.'

It was a female voice, young and bored.

'Is Chester there?'

'No.'

Jack closed his eyes. 'Will he be back today?'

'Maybe. I think.'

'But you don't know?'

Silence.

'Okay, could you tell him that Jack called, please?'

'Hang on, I think he's just come in.'

Jack listened to muffled voices. The phone crackled, like it was being held against a chest. Then Jack could hear Chester swearing: ' … well for fuck's sake, when can you work?'

The voice that had answered the phone trailed away. Jack could not make out what it was saying. 'Hello?' he said.

Chester's voice, irate: 'What?'

'That's nice. Do you train your staff in phone etiquette?'

'Oh, it's you. Jesus, fucking uni students! They're all desperate for casual work but when you give them a job, they're never available! Can't work Tuesday afternoons. Okay, what about Wednesday? No. Thursday? Yeah, but only for twenty minutes in the morning. Great. Weekends? No. That's when I wash my dog's arsehole! Un-fucking-believable!'

'Maybe it's just you. Have you been using deodorant like I told you?'

'Ha ha.'

'What do you need a casual for anyway?'

'I do have another life, Susko. Unlike yourself.'

'Masturbation doesn't count for another life,' said Jack. 'What else you got?'

Sinclair's voice grew more irritated, grinding up through the gears like an eighteen-wheeler. 'What have I got?' he said, almost snarling down the phone. 'About a dozen Edward Kass books that you want, *muchacho*. That's what I got!'

'Now, now. Just because the pretty uni students don't want to sleep with the big fat boss is no reason to take it out on me.'

Chester sighed into the phone. 'Do people hit you a lot, Susko?'

'Of late, or just in general?'

'Okay, whatever. I've got 'em, you want 'em. If you don't want 'em, I know someone else who does. *Comprende?*'

Jack put a thumb in behind his belt buckle and carefully adjusted his jeans. It was time for another painkiller. 'You learning Spanish, Sinclair? You need to work on your accent.'

Silence. 'Twenty-five dollars each. And I'm not going to bargain. I've got a woman who's willing to pay. I told her that I'd let her know today. Today's getting old.'

'A woman?' Jack frowned. 'What's her name?'

'That'd cost you another twenty-five bucks.'

Jack pressed a couple of fingers to his forehead and rubbed between his eyes in small, tight circles. Then he looked up at the damp-stained ceiling. 'How about I take a guess,' he said, getting a little steamed. He kicked a piece of broken mug on the floor. 'Celia Mitten sound about right?'

No reply.

Jack asked in a stern voice: 'When did you speak to her?'

'She rang this morning. How did you know?'

'You sent her to me, Einstein. Yesterday.'

'Really? That was her? I didn't recognise her voice.' There was the sound of fingers drumming wood. Then in a sly voice, he asked: 'What's her story?'

Jack was not going to tell Chester she was Kass's daughter. 'Another fan,' he said, vaguely.

'Well then, so there's more than one buyer out there,' replied Chester, his haughty tone returning. 'So it's either you or her, Susko. What's it going to be? The clock is ticking.'

Jack carefully straightened his back, feeling the bandage on his wound pull at his skin. With the pain came a reminder of the previous night. 'Anyone else been interested?'

'Only the phone call last week, some guy who didn't leave a name. I already told you that.'

'Yeah, you did.' Jack scribbled in a corner of the address book. 'So where'd you get a dozen Edward Kass books?'

'I have my contacts. And it's exactly eleven copies. That's two hundred and seventy-five dollars.'

'They better not have State Library of New South Wales stamped in them.'

'I run a legitimate business, Susko. You're the one who used to drive a criminal around.'

'Careful I don't ask him for a favour,' said Jack, regretting he had ever mentioned Ziggy Brandt to Sinclair. 'Where did you get them?' he repeated.

Chester blew a raspberry into the phone. 'Two hundred and seventy-five dollars.'

Jack dragged the phone along the counter and eased himself into a chair beside his desk. There was white powder all over it where the police had dusted for prints. He was careful not to get any on the sleeves of his jacket.

'Two seventy-five is too rich,' he said, calmly.

'Don't give me that crap! I told you, if you don't want them, that's fine by me. It's non-negotiable. End of story.'

Jack had to be careful. Even Chester had his limits. 'I don't believe Celia Mitten would pay twenty-five per book, Sinclair,' he said.

'Oh, really?'

'Yeah, really. If she were willing to pay you twenty-five, there's no way you'd offer them to me at the same price.'

Chester grunted. 'Maybe I like you,' he offered, trying to regain some control. 'Don't waste your window of opportunity. There's about sixty seconds left.'

'I wouldn't waste yours,' replied Jack, smoothly. 'Because you're not getting twenty-five from me.'

Chester laughed. 'No skin off my ball sack, Jack. I'll get it out of our Miss Celia instead.'

Jack picked up a lighter and flicked a flame from it. He stared at it for a moment. 'Did she say why she wanted them?'

'Who cares?'

'Right.'

'Well?' said Chester. 'I'm waiting.'

'Someone's just come in, I'll call you back, okay?'

'Don't make me wait, Susko. You can think what you like. I'm calling her at exactly five o'clock, Eastern Standard Time. It stands at twenty-five per book. You or her.'

Jack rubbed a pinch of police powder between his fingertips. Chester's voice had lost some heat. 'Let me think about it,' said Jack.

'*Adios amigo.*'

Jack took out his wallet and found Celia Mitten's card. He checked her address. Reporting the damaged door to the insurance company could wait until tomorrow.

Jack caught a train from Town Hall to Kings Cross. Regardless of its newly paved footpaths and bronze historical plaques, the Cross still smelled of takeaway food and stale beer. He walked through, past the tired strip-show joints and bars, the souvenir shops and greasy-windowed liquor outlets, the McDonald's where a guy stood out front and spilled the contents of a hamburger over the footpath as he tried to stick it in his mouth. Then past the fruit vendor who never had to worry about the homeless stealing his apples. He got to the chlorine-laced fountain and continued along Macleay Street.

Within twenty metres, everything changed: neighbouring Potts Point was the Manhattan of Sydney, or so the real-estate guides said. Art-deco apartment blocks, delicatessens with twelve-dollar sandwiches, and flashy cars swinging out of underground parking. Lots of actors and film people around, too: the successful having their lunch, the struggling serving the macchiatos. Naked plane trees lined the length of Macleay Street, looking like up-ended roots washed of soil, unreal and majestic. As Jack walked, the wind picked up the odd browned leaf from a roof gutter and tossed it down, fluttering in gentle swirls across the street. Brass railings and doorknobs and marble entrances shone. Jack liked it. Pity all he could afford there was a walk.

Celia's Crystal Palace was on the ground floor of the Macleay Regis building. It sparkled between an antique furniture shop and a florist. From across the road, Jack scanned the front window, bright with bracelets and earrings and tiaras. He could not see if anybody was inside. Jack hoped his visit was not going to be a waste of time. When he saw Ian Durst step out through the front door, he was pretty sure that was not going to be the case.

Jack watched Durst pull his coat tighter and shrug his shoulders at the cold. It was a nice-looking coat. It was probably very warm. Durst took notice of a new Bentley Continental GT coupe coming around the corner out of Challis Avenue. As it drove by he pulled a scarf from his coat pocket and wrapped it around his neck. Then he began walking up the street, in the direction of Kings Cross, blowing into his cupped hands and rubbing them vigorously together.

Jack stepped off the footpath and stood between two parked cars. He kept his eyes on Durst. He watched him check his suntanned reflection in a window. As Durst adjusted his scarf, Jack crossed the street. He stopped opposite the front door of Celia's shop. Durst continued on. Then he got into the driver's side of a parked car. Jack waited a few moments to hear the sound of the engine and see the car pulling out, but the white BMW stayed where it was. Jack could just make out Durst's silhouette through the rear window. He waited some more but the car did not start up. Maybe Durst was fixing his hair in the rear-view mirror. Maybe he would be a while.

Jack pushed the door to Celia's Crystal Palace open. A bell rang, shaking out a sprinkle of nostalgia. Celia Mitten looked up from behind a glass counter where she sat next to a credit card terminal, holding a pen. The machine was printing out a smooth spool of white paper.

'Mr Susko!'

'Not too busy, are you?' Jack gave a quick smile but studied her face like a poker player.

'No, not at all.' She stood up and began to clear the glass counter of invoices, a calculator and some change. 'Two minutes from closing time, actually.'

Jack glanced at his watch: nearly 4.00 p.m. Her voice

sounded a little nervous. Or was Jack listening too hard? He unbuttoned his coat.

'I'm surprised to see you,' she said. 'How are you feeling now? What actually happened?' She sounded sincere enough.

'I'm fine. It just looks bad.'

Celia waited for more.

'Bar-room altercation,' said Jack, turning away. 'Serves me right. How's your father?'

'He's better, thank you.' She tore the ribbon of paper from the eftpos machine and folded it once. Then she picked up a stapler and snapped it crisply on the corner of a couple of receipts.

'That's good to hear.' Jack looked around the shop. It was very bright in there. Two display walls were mirrored, the shelving was glass, and the colour scheme was white, bronze and silver. Jack could see bits of himself reflected all over the place. There were a hundred and one configurations of crystal stones and beads on display. For guidance, there were some pictures of women wearing different styles of tiaras, jewelled hair combs and stickpins. Everything a young princess could want and did not need to insure.

'You must be relieved,' he added.

'Oh, I can't tell you.' Celia kept her eyes down, scooping up the rest of the change spread out on the counter. She poured it back into the tray of an open till.

'Is he at home now?'

'Um, yes.' She looked up. Her eyes seemed a little bloodshot. Jack held them. She blinked a few times and then returned her attention to the counter. Her neck had flushed.

'I'd love to meet him.'

Celia shook her head in a disappointed manner. She shoved the calculator and a notepad into a drawer and closed it roughly. 'You still don't believe me about the burnt books, do you, Mr Susko?'

Jack inspected a row of brooches. 'Hammond Kasprowicz certainly didn't.'

Celia closed her eyes: a moment later she fixed them on Jack, narrowed and fiery. 'I could have told you that.'

'I was hoping we could have that cup of tea you offered.'

'My father is recuperating,' she said, irritated. 'He's fragile at the moment.' She walked out from behind the counter and stopped by the front door. She reached up to a small bank of switches and killed the lights. 'I'm sorry, but I do have to close up now.'

Jack put his hands inside his coat pockets. The sign on the front door said closing time was 5.00 p.m.

'Early today?'

'Yes, that's right.'

'Meeting someone?'

Celia went back around the counter. She picked up her red coat and handbag and came out again. She put both items down on a glass cabinet and started looking through her bag.

'I have an appointment,' she said.

'What about tomorrow?' he said, in a warmer voice. 'I'm keen to hear what your father has to say.'

Celia found her keys. Then she pulled out a mobile phone and zipped up the handbag. 'Tomorrow?' She stared at the screen of the mobile, pushing a few buttons with her thumb. Then she looked up and sighed through a begrudging smile. 'Yes, okay, Mr Susko, I think that should be fine. You could meet me here.'

'Four or five?'

'I close at five, Mr Susko.' She picked up her things. 'Please don't think me rude.'

Jack gave her a half-dejected face. 'And to think I stayed open for you.'

Celia ignored him and walked to the front door, slipping on her coat. Jack followed and she let him out. As she secured the lock he glanced up the street: Durst's car was still there.

Celia turned, hooking the handbag over her shoulder. 'So you asked him then?' she said. 'Kasprowicz?'

Jack nodded.

Celia sighed at the traffic over his shoulder. 'Well. Tomorrow then. And you can ask my father, too. Maybe you'll change your mind about things.' She gave him a weak smile and began walking away.

The air was icy and the sun had nothing left in it this late in the day. Jack crossed Macleay Street. There was a café just up the road. He sat down at an outside table and pulled out his cigarettes. He watched Celia Mitten walk by the plane trees. He noticed her glance over her shoulder. A waiter came over with pad and pen. 'Short black, thanks.'

He saw Celia stop beside Durst's BMW. She looked back along the street and then climbed into the passenger side. Jack blew some smoke and nodded to himself. Anybody watching might have said he looked like a man who knew what was going on. They would have been wrong.

~*12*~

For a windy Wednesday morning, Susko Books was doing all right. It was only 11.15 and already about a dozen people had been through. Three were browsing now. Maybe today was International Day of Second-hand Books. Or the stars were aligned just so. Any other time it might have put Jack on the road to a good mood. But a few bruises, some stitches and a busted door ensured Mr Positive was only peeking through the venetian blinds.

A customer approached the counter. She handed Jack ten dollars and a faded, hardback copy of *The Tibetan Book of Living and Dying*.

'The butler did it,' said Jack. The woman gave him a puzzled look. Small, dull metal rings pierced her nose, bottom lip and left eyebrow. She had the kind of face that did not need all the extra attention. White-wired miniature headphones were packed tightly into her ears: music buzzed faintly from them. She took her book, turned and walked out.

Jack slipped the ten dollars into the cash draw. Beside it on the counter was a scrap of paper with a few numbers and sums written on it. Chester Sinclair had accepted Jack's offer of twenty dollars per book. Minus Sinclair's twenty, and the four books he still needed for the advance Kasprowicz had paid him, Jack was left with an extra one hundred and thirty dollars. If he could squeeze a delivery fee out of the old guy, that made one hundred and eighty.

Jack stared at the figure he had written down. A shitty one eighty. It looked a little thin. In the orbit of embarrassing. Replacing the rear door would be twice that, if not more. And what about the cost of being knifed? Maybe Jack had taken his quality customer service a little too far.

He picked up a dictionary on the counter that a customer had finally decided not to buy. It was the *Concise Oxford*, tenth edition, minus dust jacket. Jack closed his eyes and thought: *Money*. He pressed a finger firmly on the page. He opened his eyes.

doldrums/ • **pl. n. (the doldrums) 1** a state of stagnation or depression. **2** an equatorial region of the Atlantic Ocean with calms, sudden storms, and light unpredictable winds.

'What are you looking up, Jack? Prior record?' Detective Peterson slapped the edge of the counter with his fingertips. He grinned, pleased with himself for being so funny. He leaned over and tried to get a look at the page Jack was holding open.

'Isn't that two words, Detective?' Jack closed the dictionary and spun it around, pushing it towards Peterson. 'Here,' he said. 'Ever used one of these before?'

The detective picked up the book and weighed it in his hand, swinging it gently up and down. He stared at the cover and nodded as though impressed. 'How about two more words?' he said. 'Insurance and fraud. Reckon they're in there as well?'

Jack noticed a customer glance over from the biography section. Cops were never good for business. Just like the past was never any good to the present.

Detective Peterson threw the book onto the counter. 'Two thousand and four,' he said, raising his voice. 'An S-Class Mercedes Benz. Black and brand new. Nice car. Remember it?'

Jack remembered. It was the kind of car heavyweight German Chancellors got driven around in. Or Sydney bigwigs who liked a lot of leg room in the back seat. 'No,' he said.

Peterson put his hands in his pockets and looked around the shop. The polyester in his blue suit crackled with static electricity. He nodded at the customer in the biography section: the man quickly resumed reading the book in his hands.

'Jerry can, bonfire, a certain Ziggy Brandt?' said Peterson, casually, like he was reading a shopping list. 'No?'

'Movie or book?'

'You were arrested, weren't you, Jack?' Peterson tilted his head and read the spines on a bookcase beside the counter. 'Down in Watson's Bay, wasn't it?'

'Nice place at the wrong time.'

'Spent a night in the cells. Didn't smell too good in there, did it?'

Jack crossed his arms and nodded at the dictionary. 'I got a word for you. How about harassment? And then maybe you could look up lawyer.'

'Just talking, aren't we?'

'The bullshit section is down the back.'

Detective Peterson scowled. He straightened up, stepped slowly to the counter. Then he reached over and flipped open the dictionary. He grinned as he ran a finger down the page. 'Ziggy Brandt didn't hesitate turning you over, eh? What'd you do, Jack? Try it on with his little girl?'

Jack shook his head. 'I was acquitted of all charges, *Geoff*. Or didn't you read that bit of the report? Got sleepy trying to concentrate on all the big words?'

Peterson smiled. 'She was a looker, wasn't she? Big tits, I remember. But daddy's little girl in the end. Claudia? Yeah, that was it. Claudia Brandt.'

The front door opened and another customer came in, a middle-aged woman with spiky hair, pink-framed glasses and large earrings. She smiled at them both and began inspecting some books laid out on a table: the discount specials, nothing over five dollars.

'I'd appreciate if you'd watch your language,' said Jack.

The detective gave him a look the equivalent of an eye gouge. 'Don't think I believe what's in that report, Susko. Nobody clean ever worked for Ziggy Brandt.'

Jack picked up his lighter, turned it around in his hand. Almost true: nobody *stayed* clean working for Ziggy Brandt. Being in his employ was a matter of how long you could go without taking a bath.

'You must have heard some interesting things driving that prick around,' added Peterson, almost jealously, glancing at the woman who had just walked in.

'Yeah. All on tape, too. Shall we do a deal?'

Ziggy Brandt was a self-made man. He was short and dark and ugly. Among other things, a property developer. He began his career with a company that provided scaffolding for high-rise projects. Most of the scaffolding he had conveniently found while walking around the city late at night — just minding his own business. One scaffold pipe at a time and the odd insurance scam and up the ladder he went. By the time Jack got the job driving his Mercedes, he was worth a cool fifty mill. On the books, that is. He was generous with cash bonuses, but you had to be available around the clock. Jack was about to throw it in when he met the daughter. He stayed on. She was impressive. Did the odd underwear catalogue while she finished her law degree. Appreciated the finer things and was happy to pay for dinner. But in the end, she cleaned out his heart like a pickpocket and left him standing with no bus fare home.

'How's your friend with the knife? Been back to check up on you?' said Peterson.

'He's already in Mexico. We're meeting in Switzerland as soon as the insurance company pays out on my door. Nothing like a lump sum to set you up for life.' Jack moved out from behind the counter and walked to the front door.

He stood there and held it open. 'I'm really very busy, Geoff.'

Detective Peterson did not move. He reached out and smoothed the pages of the dictionary still lying open on the counter. Then he turned and slowly made his way over. He stopped beside Jack at the front door.

'So why'd he pull the knife?' he asked, eyes bright with conspiracy. 'You get nervous, try and pull out of the deal? Ran down here to stop him sending it all up in flames?' He glanced around the shop. 'Just love the books too much, huh?'

'What are you talking about?' Jack tried to contain a worried look but it tightened the muscles in his face.

Peterson did not seem to notice. 'Brandt must have shown you a few tricks. His businesses burn down every month.'

'Yeah, that's it,' said Jack, without looking at him. He let go the door and walked back to the counter. Peterson stepped outside. The door closed with a soft thud. Jack looked up and saw the detective through the glass, grinning and waving goodbye.

He smiled back, whispering through his teeth: 'Fuck you, Geoff.'

Lunchtime in Double Bay. The sun was sharp and the cold air whipped canvas awnings in violent gusts. Traffic lights shook like TV antennas. Jack got off the bus and cut through Knox Street on the way to Cumberland Gardens, feeling the blood turn blue in his veins. Nobody braved the outside tables: inside, old ladies with grey bouffant hairdos and their forty-five-year-old daughters with not much to do complained and wondered if the council could do something about the wind.

Apart from that, the place was empty. Jack walked briskly. He turned down Bay Street and wondered if Annabelle would be at the house.

In his bag were the Kass books he had been able to find since delivering the first lot exactly a week ago. Jack was still in two minds about whether he should hand them over. A lot had happened in the last seven days. The books might be his only bargaining power: though for what, he had no idea. It would all depend on what Kasprowicz had to say for himself.

The long green gate was open. Jack walked through, noticing again how shabby the front yard looked. Annabelle's Audi was parked in the carport. He went up the three front steps to the house, crossed the verandah and knocked.

After a few moments, she opened it, trailing a white cloth napkin in her hand. 'Well, Mr Susko. This is a surprise. Are you collecting for a charity?'

Jack smiled. She was dressed in an oversized black jumper stretching down to her thighs and light grey tights: on her feet, thick white socks. She looked warm and very comfortable. Her hair was loose and tucked in behind her ears. No jewellery, no make-up, clear skin, smooth complexion: the effect was almost rude. The kind of woman who started wars and religious cults.

'Nice beanie,' she said. 'Did your mother knit it?'

'In case of Sydney blizzards.'

She looked Jack up and down, grinned. 'Yes, I can see it now. Bit of a mummy's boy.'

'I visit every Christmas.'

'What else could a mother want?' Annabelle stepped aside. 'Come in. You've just caught me having my lunch.'

Pity it wasn't a bath. Jack walked through. He waited for her to close the door and then followed her down the hall, into the kitchen.

'Your father not here?' he asked, watching her walk and listening to the soft, padded sound of her feet on the hall runner.

'No. Did you want to see him?'

'We had an appointment for one o'clock.'

'He's in Hong Kong on business. Don't think he'll get here in time.'

'Right.' Jack thought about getting angry, but the feeling had nothing to grab. Other feelings were grabbing hold of other things.

Annabelle dropped her napkin onto the kitchen table. 'Are you hungry?' she said, turning to Jack. 'I made too much.'

Jack noticed a bottle of Semillon, about one-third full, standing guard beside a green salad. Looked like Annabelle had opened her innings already.

'Thanks, I'm fine. Don't let me stop you.'

'I've had enough. Wine? Or Scotch, maybe? It's after twelve.'

'I'll have what you're having.'

'Easy.' She reached up to a cupboard, opened it and removed a bottle of Scotch and two glasses. Jack watched her pour generous portions. He put his bag down beside a chair and then removed his beanie, coat and scarf.

'So, more developments?' she said, turning around with

the glasses. She walked over, handed one to Jack. 'I suppose you've been talking to Celia again?'

He noticed the edge in her tone. 'This afternoon, actually. I'm meeting her father, too. Hopefully he'll be there.'

'Ah, the dark poet.'

Jack smiled. He leaned back against one of the dining chairs. 'So what's big Hammond got against him?'

'What hasn't he got against him.' Annabelle sipped her drink. She tilted her head slightly to the side and gave Jack a questioning look. 'Do you mind if I ask what happened to your face?'

'I was hoping your old man might be able to tell me.'

'What do you mean?'

Jack knew the concern on Annabelle's face was not for him. But the chance that it was, even just a little, nudged him in the ribs. He wanted to tell her what had happened. Even as he told himself to be wary, to read and consider the situation, the angles, he knew he would tell her. Given the chance, Jack realised he would always want to tell her, anything and everything.

'Somebody broke into my shop. They were trying to burn a couple of uncle Edward's books.'

'I don't understand. In your shop?'

'In my rubbish bin. Set-up job gone wrong. I turned up when I wasn't supposed to.'

Annabelle Kasprowicz looked out through the glass doors into the rear yard and frowned. Outside, the wind had tipped over a striped deckchair. 'You think my father had something to do with it?'

'Maybe.' Jack looked down and swirled the glass in his

hands. 'He denied it on the phone.'

'That's why you wanted to speak with him?'

'Yes. Nice of him to tell me about Hong Kong.'

'It was out of the blue. I made the appointment for him.' Annabelle ran a hand through her hair, thinking. Her eyes darted along the grooves between the terracotta tiles on the floor. Jack was disappointed she had lost interest in his face. 'Couldn't be helped,' she said, more to herself.

'So you earn your keep then?'

Annabelle reached for a packet of cigarettes, lit up, tossed a cheap blue lighter onto the bench. She scratched the corner of her mouth with her little finger, pensive. 'Why would he try to set you up? He'd only be setting himself up, wouldn't he?'

'Maybe,' said Jack. He had already thought of that and knew deep down that Kasprowicz probably had nothing to do with it. But the break-in was connected to something: to Hammond Kasprowicz, to this family. And now to Jack. A knife in the guts made him practically a relation.

'Why does he want them in the first place?' he asked, firmly, remembering his anger. 'Why would he be burning them and sending them to his brother?'

Annabelle gave Jack a startled look. 'You don't know that for certain.'

'I've seen the note.'

'So what? That's not proof. And those ashes could be burnt newspapers for all you know.' She moved to the other side of the island bench, away from Jack. 'I told you not to believe anything Celia Mitten said.'

'You believed it the other night.'

Annabelle looked away.

'Why don't you give me something then?' asked Jack, with more force than he had intended. 'One little idea. Preferably true.'

Annabelle dragged on her cigarette, blew out a quick blue breath. 'I would if I had one.'

'Tell me what happened between your father and Kass. Why did he take all the money?'

'Because.'

Jack waited for an answer.

Annabelle poured more Scotch into her glass. With her back to him, she said: 'Edward Kass had an affair with my mother.'

One of the halogen lights in the ceiling died, softly, like a candle being snuffed out. Annabelle turned around and stared meaningfully at Jack. 'That enough?'

He had suspected the possibility, but hearing it surprised him. Now that it was clear, all of his assumptions shifted around a little, suddenly uncomfortable and awkward, like distant relatives at a wake. Durst flashed in his mind like a hazard light.

'Runs in the family, then?' said Jack.

'What?'

'Playing around. Six-figure imaginations and you guys still go for the one-dollar thrills.'

'Excuse me?' Annabelle straightened up.

A little blood rushed to Jack's head. Who was he getting angry at? He looked at Annabelle, tried to see what her face revealed, but could not afford the entrance ticket. Truth was, Jack was the only one-dollar thrill round at Cumberland Gardens.

'Celia must be a chip off the old block,' he said, fiddling

with the lighter in his pocket. 'I saw your ex-husband leaving the sparkle shop the other day. Or are they just good friends?'

Annabelle opened her mouth, but nothing came out. She stood frozen, her lips slightly parted, soft and full. Jack almost went over and laid one on her. But as her face darkened, he realised now was probably not a good time.

'I've got to send some faxes,' she said. She crushed her half-smoked cigarette in an ashtray. Glass in hand, she walked out of the kitchen.

Jack looked around. The house was silent. A strange feeling overcame him: it was as if he were looking at himself through the window. Standing there, in somebody's house, somebody he did not know. As though he had broken in, but now had no idea what he wanted.

He walked out into another hallway. From a nearby room on his left he could hear the beeping of office equipment. The door to the room was open. He went over and stood at the entrance. Annabelle was flicking through a small pile of paper.

Kasprowicz's study: a warm cocoon of timber, leather and books. A gas heater burnt red through fake logs. There was a chess board set up on a small table in front of it, a couple of deep sofa chairs on either side, perfectly aligned. Jack scanned the bookshelves, thick with brown, black and maroon spines, all carefully lined up, every edge flush with its neighbour. He wondered if they had ever been taken down. White lace curtains filtered damp light in through a tall bay window, just behind a dark-stained desk that looked big enough to live in.

Annabelle sat behind the desk in her father's thickly

padded, green leather chair. She was turned to her left, feeding a page through the fax machine. Her eyes were wet but her expression gave nothing away.

'Kass went to hospital the other night,' said Jack. 'After getting more ashes in the mail. Thought he was having a heart attack.' He walked into the study, half-closing the door behind him.

'We've all got to go sometime.'

'True. But we don't need help to get there.'

'Everybody needs help.'

Annabelle stood up. As she reached for her glass of Scotch, Jack grabbed her wrist and drew her to him. She did not resist.

~13~

Jack Susko had never fucked in a four-thousand-dollar leather chair before. Not with the wind whipping cold rain against the window outside and the mid-afternoon light discreet and a fake-log fireplace keeping his kidneys warm. He guessed it was just one of those days and decided not to think about it too much. Better to wallow in the after-glow. To think was to let the future in and Jack was in no hurry to get there any time soon.

So he went through everything again in his mind, tried to separate events into distinct moments: stretch them out, prolong the pleasure. They had kissed hungrily. They had ripped each other's clothing off. Jack had even forgotten about his ten-odd stitches, until he lifted his arms as

Annabelle pulled off his shirt and felt a hot tightness there and groaned with the pain. She had kissed around the wound, her warm hands against his hips. 'You'd better sit back,' she had said. 'Let me take care of everything.'

Jack turned and watched a naked Annabelle Kasprowicz walk back into her father's study, a bottle of Scotch in one hand and a pack of cigarettes in the other. He made a mental note to sacrifice a small animal to the God of Afternoon Delight when he got home. Maybe Lois could nab him something suitable out in the rear yard.

He sat in one of the sofa chairs beside the small chess table, directly in front of the gas heater, warming his feet. He was wearing his jeans now, unbuttoned over the knife-cut, but nothing else. Annabelle poured some drinks: he stretched his legs before him and sank deeper into the plush velour padding of the chair. She handed him a Scotch and then searched around the floor for her clothes.

'Oh, it's cold now!' She found her tights, socks and jumper and quickly dragged them on. She did not bother with her bra. 'What's the time?'

'I don't know,' said Jack, giving a moment's thought to his business empire: but some things *were* better than money. Sometimes. 'Who cares?'

'My daughter might, that's all.'

Jack drank. As much as he wanted the afternoon to last, the world was already slipping in under the door like a draught. He stared at the perfect, neatly piled fake logs covering the gas flame of the heater, and drank some more.

Annabelle sat down on the edge of the chess table in front of him and lit a cigarette. Her cheeks were flushed. She smiled at him briefly, poured something warm from her eyes into Jack's own: but it only lasted a second or two. He reached out and put his hand on her leg, squeezed, remembered. She put her hand on his, without looking at him, squeezed back and then stood up. She turned her butt to the heater.

'What time is she due?' asked Jack.

'Four.'

'Her father dropping her off?'

'Yes.'

Jack reached for the cigarette pack. They were back in the real world again and it was overrated. He slid out a smoke, dropped the pack and then reached for one of the huge chess pieces on the board in front of him: the white knight. It looked hand-carved, all strong edges and rough broad planes, and felt as heavy as a brick.

'Do you think he's having an affair with Celia?'

'Probably. He can't help himself.'

Outside the rain was heavier and the wind blew it against the window. Jack sat forward in his chair and lit his cigarette. He was starting to feel a little colder now, too.

'Must be hard, sharing a daughter,' he said, sympathetically. 'Always seeing him.'

'Ever been to hell?'

Jack wanted to ask her what she had seen in him in the first place. Dicks like Durst were so obvious. He was an affront to average intelligence. That Annabelle might actually have loved him once ...

'Jack, I—'

'What?'

She covered her face with her hands. The cigarette burnt between her fingers. Jack stood up, took the cigarette and put his arms around her. It was then that he noticed the typewriter in the opposite corner, sitting on a small table tucked into an alcove between a bookshelf and the door. It looked like a restored antique, glossy black and immaculate. He remembered the note Celia had shown him.

Annabelle put her hands on Jack's chest. She pushed away from him. Her eyes were porcelain. 'You don't understand,' she said. 'He's destroying my life. He won't leave me alone, he rings me ten times a day. Two o'clock, three o'clock in the morning!'

'Is he threatening you?'

She looked away. 'No. Not directly.'

'What does he want?' Jack let her go.

She sat down in one of the sofa chairs and stared into the fake logs of the heater. 'He says we have to get back together, because of Louisa. That if I don't it'll ruin her life and it'll be my fault. And that he'll take her away.' She looked up at Jack. 'But it's just about the money. That's all he really wants.' Her eyes went through him, through the wall of the study, too, outside into the wind and rain. 'It's all anyone wants in this fucking family.'

'Celia, too?' Jack smoked, tapped the cigarette in an ashtray.

'Of course, Celia! What do you think?'

Jack was thinking a lot of things. All at once. It was like keeping track of white paper blowing around in a snowstorm.

'Who knows what she's up to with Ian,' said Annabelle, reaching for her Scotch.

For a moment Jack had to remember Ian was Durst. 'Does he have any claim on your money?'

'Not all of it. A lot is tied up in trusts through my father's business. But it's guaranteed he'll contest the outcome of the divorce. And he'll use Louisa against me, just like he's already using her. I know he'll drag all our shit out into the open, make me look like a terrible mother.' Annabelle stared into her drink. 'I don't want to lose my daughter.'

Silence, except for the rain against the window and the faint hiss of the gas heater. Jack scanned the floor for his clothes, saw his crisp black shirt, now crumpled on the floor near the desk.

'You said you were seeing Celia this afternoon?' said Annabelle.

'Yes.'

'Can you ... find out ... what she's up to with Ian?'

'I can try.'

For a moment Annabelle stared at the chess pieces before her. She let out a breath through her nostrils, almost a huff. A sliver of light glinted in her eyes, then she blinked and the sparks died. Something else was on her mind, too.

'Don't believe anything Edward Kass tells you, either,' she said.

There was probably more family love in a wasp's nest than around these people. 'When did the affair happen?'

A pause. 'First time was in the sixties.' Annabelle almost sounded relieved to say it. 'Mum actually left Dad and went to live with Edward. I'm not sure of the details. I hadn't been born. She came back, of course, but then it happened again later.'

'About the time your father took Kass to court.'

'Yes.'

'That was a while ago now. Why all the sudden interest?' Jack glanced at the typewriter in the corner.

'I don't know!' said Annabelle, looking up at him with cool brown eyes. 'I don't know what's going on. My father hardly ever speaks to me anymore.'

Hammond Kasprowicz had probably never been up for Father of the Year. 'When was the last time you saw Kass?'

Annabelle sighed. 'Probably on my eighteenth birthday. He gave me a poem. I still remember. It was called *In Demons Land*.'

'Nice,' said Jack. 'Just what every eighteen-year-old girl would want.'

'My father bought me a car.'

Jack was surprised it was not a pony. He went and picked up his shirt and returned to stand in front of the heater as he put it on.

'Thank you, Jack.' She stood up. 'There's nobody else I can talk to about all this.' She put a hand on his chest. Then she held a finger to his lips. Jack bit it, lightly. She pressed herself against him, unbuttoning the one button he had managed to do up.

'When can I see you again?' she asked.

'My wife's out tonight. Tango lessons. Any time after seven is clear.'

She smiled. Slipped a hand down Jack's back, slowly. Parted her lips and tilted her head and kissed him.

On the bus to Kings Cross, Jack searched through the Edward Kass books in his bag for the poem Kass had given Annabelle. He found it in *Entropy House*. The singed copy.

Page 19.

IN DEMONS LAND

His forehead smeared with defeat,
His journey without reason, willed —
The young man turned at the bridge
And shouted his commands.

Her arms broke the day,
The highest steps too splendid
For the eyes. Ten centuries
Blown about — their weight

The sin of pride. Only God
Satisfied, among the dead,
The price of empty glory faded,
And then crawled on

In exile with a myrtle crown. The light
Observed brilliant in the same,
And three mirrors the whiteness of the moon —
Another sphere proceeds the truth

You seek. Mandatory, to slake
The great awe.
Suffer the world rejoiced.
I am obedient too late.

Jack closed the book and slipped it back into his bag.
The ancient Egyptians said that when you died, the god

Ra weighed your heart against a feather, on a set of golden scales. If it were lighter, then heaven awaited. During their meeting, Edward Kass was going to have to hope for a feather the size of New Zealand.

The boss was behind the counter at Celia's Crystal Palace, head down over the till, counting out the fifties. Her lips moved silently. There were more golden notes than Jack saw in a month. Maybe he should make the switch to designer costume jewellery.

'Lucky I'm not wearing a balaclava.'

Celia looked up, surprised, and pushed the till shut. The faint sound of a bell echoed from it. A few fifties were still scrunched in her hand.

'I didn't hear you.'

'The papers call me the Phantom.'

Celia smiled. 'I'll just put this away in the safe.' She bent down below the counter. Jack heard a few digital-sounding beeps, a metallic creak, and then the hollow thud of the safe door banging shut.

'Right. Shall we go?'

'After you.'

She came out from behind the counter and went over to a large mirror: it opened to reveal a cupboard. She took out a grey woollen coat and worked her shoulders into it. Then she looked into the mirror and removed her sparkly earrings, fixed a black woollen beret on her head and teased her fringe a couple of times. 'It's just down the road. Only take a minute.'

Jack waited while she wrote something on a small piece

of paper and then taped it to the glass of the front door. She let Jack through and then followed him outside.

'Boy, it's cold today!'

'Arctic,' said Jack.

'I love it. Winter's my favourite season. And autumn as well. The cooler months.'

Jack believed her. Any excuse for more wool.

Celia moved to the edge of the road and pointed. 'It's just down there.' They crossed Macleay Street and headed in the direction of Woolloomooloo. 'We're in St Neot Avenue.'

'Wonder what he's the saint of,' said Jack.

'Poets, probably.'

'He must have suffered terribly.'

'It's only appropriate, then.' Celia's tone hardened. She quickened her pace.

Jack followed, half a step behind. 'Is your father feeling better?'

'He's working, I suppose.'

'No more packages in the mail?'

'Maybe there's one waiting now.'

'Phone calls?' Jack paused. 'Visitors?'

'Just you, Mr Susko.'

They walked on. Questions were crowding Jack's frontal lobe. Questions about Durst, about Kasprowicz, about Celia, too. It made him frown. So did the guy who walked past wearing designer-ripped jeans, a bleached red T-shirt, scarf, sunglasses, thongs and a takeaway latte.

They turned into St Neot Avenue, following the long curve of an apartment block on the corner. Cars lined either side of the street, bumper to bumper all the way down. Lots of trees, too, and small front yards with manicured hedges and lawns and potted plants. It looked like an expensive stretch of real estate. Every building was an apartment block, in a range of architectural styles. Across the road, Jack noticed a renovated art-deco number with a column-framed entrance and a couple of palm trees out front. It even had a name: Grantham. But that was not where Edward Kass lived.

Celia stopped in front of a plain, redbrick low-rise opposite. Its name was simply *Twenty-One*.

'This is it,' she said.

The path leading to the entrance was of pale blue-and-yellow-tinted stone. Hedges on either side added to the shadows thrown by a large frangipani tree that grew in a small patch of grass, half-naked and slightly obscene with its blunt, sausage-like branches. Jack shivered for a second as he went up the three front steps: under the entrance awning it was dark and the cold was palpable, as if he had walked into a butcher's coolroom. He looked through the glass doors into the foyer, but inside it was dark too, and did not look much warmer. Dank was the word that came to mind.

Celia slid a key into the lock and pushed the door open. The place smelt like closed windows and cheap carpet cleaner. She pressed a switch on the wall: the lights came on in the stairwell with a lazy *clunk*. Jack looked around. Maroon carpet, wood-veneer walls and a bit of dull brass here and there. And a sulking pot plant that looked like it needed a holiday. They began to climb the stairs, under weak yellow light that would have made an athlete look sick. Not a sound but the odd creaking step, or the banister giving a little. Somehow, the place suited Jack's idea of Kass: moody, mostly cranky and never happy with visitors. Then again, the place was probably all he could afford after coming out the tight end of a family fortune.

The apartment was on the first floor. The front door was slightly open. Celia gave a puzzled look as she pushed it open.

'Hello? Dad?'

Jack walked in behind her. The place was dark: green curtains on two windows were drawn, filtering a weak, four-o'clock light into the room. A lamp in the corner glowed dimly and the ceiling light drizzled down at about twenty-five watts. Two large, dark green lounge chairs with wide armrests and wood-grain edging kept each other company. The room was crowded with furniture and bookshelves and the walls were covered in pictures.

'Dad?'

Jack looked around. Without thinking, he sniffed the air: something strong, sulphurous. Something wrong. Instinctively, he took a step backwards, as if any second he might have to make a run for it. The whole room seemed to grow darker, and smaller, seemed to shrink in around him like a child's fairytale nightmare.

Celia slipped off her coat. 'Is anybody here?'

There was a noise, like something being knocked over. Jack and Celia turned towards the doorway opposite. Ian Durst walked into the room. There was blood on his white shirt, patchy streaks where a hand had gripped or pulled or wiped itself. And he was holding a gun. The way his shoulder drooped down a little told Jack that it was not made out of plastic.

~14~

CELIA MITTEN EVENTUALLY STOPPED SCREAMING. She was now sitting in one of the lounge chairs, right up on the cushion's edge, legs clamped together and to the side, every part of her shaking, all in different directions. Durst had given her a whisky that she had not yet tasted. At least it gave her something to stare at. Shock had shut her down for the moment.

Jack went into the kitchen, where Celia had just been. Durst followed him.

Edward Kass was bent forward over the kitchen table. His head rested on an open notebook and a few loose pages spread out before him. A couple of pens were there too, a cheap blue Bic and a fancy black fountain, as well as a pencil lying next to a sharpener and a small, dirty cube of rubber. His arms were crossed over his lap, hands resting palm up on each thigh. Kass looked as though he had fallen asleep—almost childlike, innocent and oblivious. Maybe he had dozed off while grinding a gear or two over the final wording of a sentence. Painful as that might have been, Jack doubted it was the cause of the hole in the side of his head.

He stepped closer to the body. Just in front of the dead man, covered in blood, a piece of paper with a line that had survived the bullet's aftermath. It read: *the waters rise around me.*

On the kitchen floor lay another body. Jack recognised that one, too. The thin man was lying on his stomach, arms tucked in under his chest, and his legs splayed a little, one leg bent awkwardly with the foot in against the knee of the other. His head was turned to the side, eyes open, blank, staring across the floor at the wall opposite: or at the void he had not long before fallen into. A bullet had darkened his back with blood that seemed as black as sump oil. It had seeped out around him and circled the top half of his body: a halo of thick, paint-like blood, rich and red against the off-white linoleum patterned with curlicues of gold and silver covering the floor. Jack had been looking forward to catching up with the guy again, telling him that attacking people with knives in their place of business was not a very nice thing to do. That playing with sharp objects and starting fires would ultimately only get him into trouble. But it looked like he already knew.

If Ian Durst remembered Jack from the other Friday, when he had thrown a fist and some BMW keys into Jack's stomach, he did not let on. He stood at the entrance to the kitchen, heavy-shouldered like he was suffering a hangover, pointing out details with one hand, while the gun hung limply in the other. That was where he had seen the intruder. That was where they had struggled, there where the chair lay knocked over. That was where the gun had fallen and then slid up against the sink cupboards for him to grab. He said how the guy had tried to knee him in the balls, scratch his eyes, even bite his nose. He went on like that for a while. Lots of details. Ian Durst seemed to be blessed with a photographic memory. Maybe disgraced former gynaecologists were good at remembering things.

Jack listened and looked around the kitchen. He was wary and nervous and kept glancing at Durst's gun hand to make sure his finger did not creep up and hug the trigger, accidentally or otherwise. Adrenaline could do funny things to nerve-endings, even after you had calmed down.

Durst said: 'I had to get out from under him after the gun went off.'

Jack watched him pull a face. His thin, leathery lips stretched tightly across his Royal Doulton teeth.

'He looks small but he weighed a ton. I had to kind of slide out. Dead weight, all right.'

'So how did he get in?' asked Jack.

'Don't know. Must've picked the lock. The door was open when I got here.'

'Pity you didn't get here earlier.'

'Yeah,' said Durst. 'Pity.' The fringe of his swept-back hair had fallen down over his forehead in two thick, Superman-like curls. He pushed them back up with his free hand, letting it rest on top of his head.

Jack looked at Edward Kass again. He could identify a

little of the man he had seen in the photo on the net: long face, thick lips, strong straight nose. The hair was grey of course, though still there, the ears larger, the eyebrows like wild tufts of bleached grass growing out of a crack in a wall. He was not so gaunt in old age, or as dark. Whatever had been on his mind, only the eyes could confirm, and they were now shut. Forever. His poetry would never be so definitive.

The dead poet was wearing a blue cardigan, an orange-and-black-checked flannelette shirt, faded black pants with folded-up cuffs and red tartan slippers. House clothes. Blood dripped onto the left slipper from the edge of the table: Jack could hear it now in the dark silence of the room, the soaked slipper, the thick *thwap ... thwap ... thwap* of slowly congealing blood dropping down, almost in slow motion. Jack had never seen a dead body before. He never thought his first time would be a double.

He looked over at the man on the floor. Shiny, silver-grey tracksuit and what looked like brand new black Adidas sneakers with gleaming white stripes. Tough-guy-in-the-money, break-and-enter clothes.

'Do you know him?' asked Durst.

Jack turned too quickly: his neck jarred and made him grimace. Ian Durst did not notice. He was staring down at the body on the floor as well—casually, half interested, like the dead man was just a hooked fish gone stiff on a jetty.

'No,' said Jack. The question annoyed him. 'Do you?'

Durst shrugged and shook his head. 'Just one of those faces, I suppose. Makes you think you've seen it before. Don't you think?'

Jack frowned. His heartbeat changed up a gear. 'Not really.'

Ian Durst locked his clear baby-blue eyes onto Jack's hazel-brown ones. Then he glanced down at the gun in his hand, but without moving his head too much. He checked it out from a couple of angles, turning it a little this way and then the other. He had an almost smug look on his face. A grin dimpled his cheek but was gone before it could be accused of anything. He looked up again, his face now hard and dark and vaguely threatening.

Jack held the stare. Said nothing. Neither did Durst.

Celia's shaken voice was heard from the lounge room. 'The police are here.'

Jack half expected to see Peterson among the blue uniforms searching the apartment for clues. He was relieved not to. Instead, a Detective Sergeant Keith Glendenning was the man in charge. Under his creased grey suit he possessed maybe half a personality. Everything else about him was pretty average, too: height, width, looks and shoes. Jack wondered about his abilities. Glendenning walked with a heavy gait, slowly and sadly, like a man who might have carried a bucket and mop for a living instead of a badge and a gun. He was probably only in his forties but looked a decade older around the eyes. They crowded in together above a nose the size of a small ham. He kept glancing at a mobile phone in his right hand, as if hoping it would ring—but it never did. Not even a text message. The disappointment on his face came and went swiftly. Jack could see it was well practised.

He gave a statement to a couple of police officers first. They asked him to come into the main bedroom. It was dark with stained timber and heavy brown drapes. The double bed was made, the polished wood-veneer closet closed, the rugs on the floor perfectly aligned: there was nothing out of place, not even a pair of old pyjamas thrown over the tall-backed chair set against the wall. Kass must have been an obsessive-compulsive it was so neat in there. One of the officers wrote down what Jack said, the other prompted him. Neither looked him in the eye, once. Cops had a way of making Jack feel that whatever he said was a lie. It must have been a trick they learnt at police school: *How to dredge your suspect's guilt, no matter if it's from when he was five and stole a chocolate bar from the corner shop.* After they had finished, he read through the script and signed.

Then Detective Sergeant Keith Glendenning had his turn. There were flakes of dandruff on his shoulders. In a steady, bored voice he asked a lot of questions. One of them was whether Jack knew either of the dead men.

'I knew Edward Kass,' said Jack. 'But only by name. This would have been our first meeting.'

'About what?'

'His books. I'm a book dealer.' Jack elevated the prestige of his business, but it had no visible effect on Detective Sergeant Glendenning. He looked just as bored as ever.

'What about his books?' he asked.

Jack cleared his throat. He knew Celia had already spoken to the detective. 'I was interested in buying them.'

'Why?'

'So I could sell them. It's what I do.'

'Are they worth a lot of money?'

'Not really.' Jack checked himself. 'Well, a little, if they're signed.'

'And that's why you were coming to see him?'

'That's right.'

'How much?'

'How much what?'

'How much are they worth? Signed.'

'Not enough to get excited about.'

Detective Sergeant Keith Glendenning gave a sly smile. Probably his first for the month. Jack caught a glimpse of his crooked, not very white teeth. The cruel shape of his pale, fleshy lips emphasised a mouth that had spoken an obscenity or two in its time. A mouth that could snarl when it wanted to.

'How much gets you excited?' asked the detective.

'Anything above a dollar eighty-five.'

Jack had the distinct feeling that maybe he had underestimated the detective. Glendenning was piling on the questions like a chess player who only moved his pawns. But before you knew it, most of them were standing around your queen, grinning like a pack of murderous dwarves.

'So they were worth enough to come and see him?' The detective's smile had vanished. He checked his mobile phone, squinting down at its illuminated screen.

Jack shrugged his shoulders, tried to give an air of calm. 'A buck's a buck. Unless you're on a copper's wage, I suppose.'

The detective looked up. 'It's only a buck over here, too, last time I checked.' The tone was nothing nasty but the hard grey-blue eyes were unimpressed. Glendenning glanced down at his mobile phone again. 'And what about the other guy, on the floor?' he asked, like it was an afterthought. Like he did not care whether Jack knew him or not.

They were standing in a small connecting hall that led to the two bedrooms in the apartment. It was dim — the bare, single globe above them did a cheap job. Jack looked at the floor: it was covered in an orange-and-brown carpet, patterned with circles and some kind of curved pyramid shape set at different angles between the circles. He doubted there was ever a time it was fashionable. As his eyes followed the pattern around for a moment, he noticed somebody else walk into the hallway.

'Just need the toilet.' Durst squeezed past Detective Sergeant Glendenning. He looked at Jack. Jack looked back. The detective noticed.

As Durst shut the door to the bathroom, Glendenning scratched the stubble on his broad chin. 'So have you ever seen him before? The guy on the floor?'

Jack casually swept the hair across his forehead, though he felt far from casual doing it. 'No.' He shook his head to emphasise the fact. The detective looked at him, one eyebrow rising ever so slightly over his left eye. Or maybe Jack was imagining things. A primary school teacher once told the young Jack Susko that his imagination was too ripe and would ultimately get him into trouble. Maybe. He smiled at the detective and shook his head a little more and gave the detective the old *Sorry I can't help you* look. But even as he shook his head and smiled his dumb smile, Jack knew that he should have come clean. He was lying to the law. The moment the word 'no' had left his mouth he knew it was a stupid move. So what the hell was he doing?

From the kitchen, somebody said: 'Jesus, what a mess.'

A toilet flushed. Ian Durst stepped out into the claustrophobic hallway again. 'Excuse me,' he said, turning sideways as he passed between Jack and the detective. They both watched him leave.

'You know him?' asked the detective, nodding in Durst's direction.

Jack's face was firm, serious. 'No,' he said. His second stupid 'no' of the day.

'Looks like you don't know too many people, Mr Susko.'

'I'm a bit of a recluse.'

'Busy book-dealing.'

'Pretty much.'

'You do a lot of reading?'

'Just before bed.'

'No girlfriend then?'

'Not any I ever wanted to wake up to.'

Detective Sergeant Glendenning gave his second smile for the financial year. One more and he would be eligible for a rebate. 'Sounds like you're too picky.'

'I live in hope. But we can't all be happily married men.'

The detective looked down at his mobile again. The smile on his face went back to wherever it had come from. Almost in a whisper, he said: 'No, we can't.' He slipped the phone into his pocket and adjusted his round shoulders. 'We'll be in touch.'

'And don't leave the country?'

No smile this time. 'We know where you live, Mr Susko. Don't worry about a thing.'

He walked out of the hall and back into the living room. Jack watched him a moment and then followed. Celia was still sitting in the lounge chair, her face pale and puffy from crying. A half-glass of water on the coffee table told Jack that she had probably been given a sedative.

Durst stood by a glass credenza full of Japanese dolls and smoked. Uniformed police officers moved back and forth across the room, all attention focused on the bodies in the kitchen.

Detective Sergeant Glendenning and a female officer approached Celia. 'That's all for the moment, Ms Mitten. Officer Ivanovic here will help you through the rest of the investigation and assist you in any way she can. She'll also organise a social worker and some trauma counselling for you. Don't hesitate to ask her for anything else.' He glanced at the officer and then back down at Celia. 'We'll need to see you at the station in the morning. I'm sorry for your loss.'

Celia looked up at the detective and nodded, pressing her bloodless lips together into a sad half-smile. Glendenning reached out and touched her on the shoulder. Behind him, another uniformed officer came in from the kitchen and moved the coffee table aside. Then a couple of ambulance officers wheeled out one of the bodies. It was Kass: an arm showed from beneath the sheet that was pulled over him. There were ink-stains on his fingertips. Celia Mitten stared at the hand.

Durst walked over from the credenza. 'Can I take her away now?'

'Yes,' replied Glendenning. 'Does she have somewhere else to stay?'

'She can stay with me.'

The detective followed the stretcher out with his eyes. 'She's stayed with you before then?' He turned to face Durst again.

A slight pause. 'No.'

'So you two aren't together?'

Durst looked down at Celia and put the cigarette to his lips and smoked. 'Yes. We're together.'

'Good,' replied the detective and walked off. As he got to the front door, he turned around again and spoke to Jack: 'You can go as well.'

'Thanks.'

The second body was wheeled out of the kitchen: the short shoplifter guy who had knifed Jack at Susko Books only three days ago. As he watched the body being manoeuvred through the lounge room, Jack's brain started to tumble out some ideas; they tried to line themselves up into some kind of order. They were not having much luck. Jack rubbed his face. Better not to think about it too much right now. Thinking always had a tendency to get out of hand.

He smiled at Celia, who did not notice, and followed the body out. He felt sorry for her. The ambulance officers paused in the hallway to tighten the belt over the dead man before descending the stairs. Jack waited and then followed. He went carefully down behind the trolley, step by step, until they reached the dim, damp lobby below. Jack was still not thinking too much. That was good.

He watched the ambulance officers pass through the front doors of the apartment building. He felt an icy rush of wind from outside and then listened to it moan as the doors closed and squeezed it out. He wound on his scarf and buttoned up his jacket and then stepped out into the dark. The ambulance officers loaded the body into an ambulance and slammed the doors. Jack watched them drive off. Nobody else about: for a moment, the world was as cold and empty as an alcoholic's refrigerator. Jack's stomach sounded a thin, hollow gurgle. He wondered if it was appropriate to think about food at such a time.

The frangipani tree near the entrance stood above him like some surreal candelabra wrought from shadows, faint against the city's glow, its ragged candles snuffed and long cold. He stared at it and shivered and then started walking away. *Christ*. That was all he needed after a heavy day: a movie-size serve of gloomy symbolism.

~15~

ANOTHER DAY. Jack was tense, stiff in the neck and aching, like he had been wearing a long wet coat all week, with anchors in the pockets. Last night he had dreamt that all his teeth fell out, that he had spat them into the palm of his hand, an endless mouthful. When he woke he had run his tongue over them a couple of times, to make sure they were still in his head. Now he sipped his coffee. He smoked a cigarette. He was sitting in the Eames chair with the heater pulled up close and his feet resting on top of it, trying to concentrate. Lois was curled up on a cushion on the floor. He was going over *connections*. Unchecked, he knew this type of mental activity often led to lunacy. But right now, it was all he had to work with. He was nervous about the connection between himself and the killer. But more than that, it was the question of who else was connected to the dead shoplifter—and why—that was making a vein in his temple pulse.

Two men dead because of half-a-dozen morbid poetry books? Not to mention the stitches in his gut.

A knock at the door. Jack groaned and got up out of the chair like a man whose woman had run off with his best friend. Maybe it was the cops. Maybe it was Detective Peterson, round for some early morning fun, having heard about the murder yesterday afternoon from his colleague. But when Jack opened the door and saw Annabelle Kasprowicz standing there, his low mood fizzed and dissolved like an aspirin.

'It would have been easier if I'd walked,' she said. Her face was bright with cold. 'I ended up parking closer to my place.'

'Maybe it'd be easier if you just moved in.'

Annabelle rolled her eyes and stepped into Jack's apartment for the first time. He closed the door behind her while she looked around. Nothing seemed to hold her attention for too long.

'It's warm,' she said.

'Make yourself at home.'

She was wearing a knee-length, jersey wrap dress with a 1970s paisley print in brown and turquoise. It did not look like it would be too difficult to remove at the end of a hard day. Her legs were held secure in tight, knee-high navy leather boots that would probably require a little more effort. The long, turquoise fine-wool scarf around her neck would pose no problem at all. A little jewellery, a little make-up, a puff of perfume. She sent every sense nuts, including the sixth.

Lois stood up, stretched and then miaowed. She sauntered over to Annabelle and turned some lazy figure eights through her legs.

'I didn't pick you for a cat lover,' said Annabelle.

'Neither did I.'

'What's his name?'

'Lois.'

'A girl? Maybe I should leave?'

'Don't worry. It's an open relationship.'

Annabelle removed her scarf. She crouched down and stroked the cat. Lois began to purr. Jack moved the heater into the centre of the living room.

'You've heard,' he said.

Annabelle looked up, continued stroking the cat. 'Ian called me last night from the police station.'

So they had taken Durst to the cop shop. Jack extinguished his cigarette. 'You don't seem too upset.'

Annabelle turned to the cat again. 'I'm shocked by what's happened, of course, but ... ' She stopped, rubbed Lois' nose. 'You know my family, Jack. You know it's fucked. I might have passed my uncle in the street and not even recognised him.' She looked up. 'I've never really known him. What else can I say?'

'Have you told your father?'

'He's not due back until tonight. I can't get him on his mobile.' She paused. 'I can't just leave a message.'

'Sure.'

Annabelle stood up, brushed cat hairs from her hands. 'So Ian caught someone breaking into the place?'

Jack nodded.

'What happened exactly?'

'Exactly, I don't know. When I got there with Celia, the door was open, Durst was wearing a blood-splattered shirt and holding a gun, and there were two bodies in the kitchen. All that was missing were lights and a camera.'

'Who was the other man?' Annabelle sat down on a red, corduroy two-seater couch.

Jack hesitated. 'I don't know.'

'Didn't the police say anything?'

'The police never say anything.' He picked up his cigarettes from the coffee table. 'What about Durst? What did he tell you?'

'Not much. The man who broke in had already shot Edward. Ian caught him going through his pockets.'

Jack put the cigarette in his mouth and struck a match. 'So Durst's definitely with Celia.'

'Looks that way.' Annabelle smiled—a second later it slipped from her face like an icicle.

'It looks a lot of ways,' muttered Jack.

Annabelle reached across for his cigarette. 'Poor Celia. She doesn't know Ian. Though maybe she deserves him.'

'You don't think it's love, then?'

'That's not even close to being funny.'

'You think he's using her?'

'Ian can't help himself. It's the way he was born.'

'Why? Just to get at you?'

She shrugged, smoked.

'I thought he wanted you back?' said Jack.

'My ex-husband is a very childish man.' Annabelle tapped the cigarette in an ashtray. 'He probably thinks it will make me jealous. And my father angry.'

'What's he got to do with it?'

'He's always hated Ian. He wants to see him disappear. No money from the settlement and no Louisa. His lawyers are very good. Poor Ian doesn't have much to fight with.'

'Why would seeing Celia annoy your father?'

'He owns Celia's business.' She drew on the cigarette, blew smoke up to the ceiling.

Jack frowned. There was always something around the corner with these people. And it always seemed to be Hammond Kasprowicz.

'Don't look so confused! Silly little games are how the world turns.'

'Your old man owns Celia Mitten's business?'

Annabelle nodded. 'Sometimes guilt can work with him. Or at least it used to. Celia possesses her own unique talents. I told you not to believe anything she said.'

'Your ex-husband goes a long way to be a pain in the arse.'

Annabelle stared at the cigarette in her hand. 'He used to be fun. Once.'

'Memories are wonderful things.'

'Are you jealous?'

'Who? Me?' Jack got up and went into the kitchen. He wished he had cracked Durst one back at Kass's apartment. He came back with a plunger of coffee and a clean cup. Nobody spoke. Plumbing thrummed in one of the walls. It seemed to go with the mood.

'I know who the other guy was,' said Jack. The words came out by themselves.

'What do you mean?'

'The guy who Durst shot, who killed your uncle. I knew him.'

Silence. Then: 'Who?'

'This guy.' Jack lifted his T-shirt, exposing the stitches just above his hip. He looked down at the wound, but not at Annabelle. Then he let go of the T-shirt and sat down in the Eames chair with his coffee. He waited for her to say something.

Annabelle continued to stare at him. 'Did you tell the police?'

'No.'

'Why?'

Jack turned and watched Lois yawn. 'Because I want to know who the hell he was working for.' He thought he might feel better for telling Annabelle. Instead, a kind of nausea drifted through him.

'You shouldn't play games with the police.'

'It's how the world turns, isn't it?' said Jack, irritated. 'Durst acted like he'd never seen me before.'

'So what? He'd just shot a man! And he's only seen you once.' Annabelle thought about it: the effort pressed faint lines into the corners of her eyes. 'What are you suggesting?'

'Nothing,' he snapped. Maybe he was thinking too much again. Maybe the connections were all just slipknots. Maybe soon enough they were going to cut off his circulation.

Annabelle went over and knelt in front of him. She cupped his face in her hands. They were warm, soft hands. 'You look tired,' she said.

'I have to get ready for work.'

'I'll drive you. Does that give you more time?'

Jack looked into her eyes, grabbed a handful of hair at the nape of her neck. She was beautiful, crazy beautiful, and he clenched his jaw and tightened his grip around the glowing hair in his fist. 'Time for what?' he said.

Annabelle half closed her eyes. She rolled her head around in a small circle, slowly, while Jack pressed his fingers into her neck. A soft sigh parted her lips. Then she put her hands on his knees and pushed herself up. She tilted her hip a little and reached around her side. She began to untie the straps on her dress.

'I didn't have time for a shower this morning,' she said. 'I feel dirty. Do you mind?'

'All I've got is a bath.'

Annabelle began to slip the dress off. 'Better let the cat out then.'

The *Concise Oxford English Dictionary* was still on the counter at Susko Books where Jack had left it the day before. He put his bag down and stared at it. He put his hand on the front cover and thought about Annabelle Kasprowicz. Then he closed his eyes, flipped the book open and stabbed a finger at the page:

poignant/ • **adj.** 1 evoking a keen sense of sadness or regret. 2 *archaic* sharp or pungent in taste or smell.

Jack closed the *OED* and returned it to its place in the reference section. Next time he would try another book.

He turned on the heat, the lights, and slipped the float in the cash drawer. He took a bite of the croissant he had bought on the way into the city and drank from a small bottle of orange juice. The shelves needed dusting. The floor needed sweeping. Jack wondered how much it would cost to employ a regular cleaner. He thought about how much he would get stung for the rear door. He wondered how long the day was going to take getting to 5.00 p.m.

When the phone started ringing, he was sure it was the police. Worst-case scenario, it would be Peterson. He answered with a tight hello.

'You going to pick these books up or what?'

It was Chester Sinclair. It was the first time Jack did not mind hearing his voice.

'Mr Sinclair. And how are we this morning?'

'Yeah, great. So when do I get my money?'

'That's wonderful. The wife, kids?'

'Have you dropped a tab, Susko?'

'Mum and dad?'

Chester paused. 'Jesus.'

'And how's business?'

'Two hundred and seventy-five dollars down. I'd like my money today. Now, fuck it.'

'What's the rush?' said Jack. 'Hot date and you need money for a nose job?' He noticed the edginess in Sinclair's voice.

'The books you wanted are here. As agreed.'

'And?'

'Come, pay, leave.'

'That's not a sentence, Sinclair. There are laws, you know.'

'Yeah, I know. They've already been here.'

'What?'

'I want nothing to do with it, so just come and get your books and that's that. Man, I had a feeling about this deal in the first place.'

Jack watched somebody peek through the glass of the front door. They had a look and then walked back up the stairs. 'Who's been there?' he asked.

'The fucking police, that's who!'

Jack let it sink in. 'Why?'

'Because your fucking poet's been shot, that's why. They were waiting here for me this morning.' Chester lowered his voice. 'I want these books out of here.'

'Why would they come and see you?' Jack's tone was cool but his blood pressure had started to climb.

'Because my fucking message was still on Kass's machine!'

'What message?'

'I rang to see if he would be interested in selling his personal copies. If I'd known the fucking police would be round here ...'

'Just relax, Sinclair. Your walnut might pop. What did they ask you?'

'What do you mean?'

Jack shook his head. 'I mean *what did the police ask you?*'

'Hey, don't come at me all smart-fuck-son-of-a-bitch! I'm allergic to the goddamn police. They make me come out in a rash and I can't shit for a month.'

'Try bran and some exercise.'

'You just come and get these books out of here.'

Jack tried again, his voice calm, friendly. 'So what did they ask you?'

'They wanted to know why I was after Kass's books.'

'What did you tell them?'

'That I'd heard on the grapevine a collector was after them.'

'And of course they asked who.'

'Yeah, they asked.'

Jack let out a slow, measured breath. He hated Chester Sinclair. It was going to be his new hobby. He was going to spend a couple of hours at it every morning, like yoga. 'And?'

Down the line, a sound of phlegm being coughed and then swallowed. 'I told them to speak to you.'

'You're a real friend, Sinclair. Next time I need a two-thousand-volt migraine, I'll give you a call.'

'Hey, what was I going to say? It's got nothing to do with me.'

Jack remained silent.

'Anyway, what have you got to worry about? Just tell them who your collector is.' The logic eased the tension in Chester's voice. His smug, confident tone returned. 'Just pass it on down the line, man, easy as that. It's not like *you* killed the bastard. You're just a guy who sells books. Like me!'

'Just like you,' said Jack in a low voice. He glanced at the clock on the wall behind him: nearly 10.00 a.m. Time to open up the shop. 'Did they say anything about the shooting?'

'No. But they wanted to see Kass's books. I told them I didn't have any.'

'Right.' It was a small lie, insignificant: not like Jack's. He was jealous.

'So you going to pick them up today?' There was a bubble of hope in Chester's voice.

Jack did not hesitate to pop it. 'What for?' he said. 'Now

that you've palmed the cops onto me, I'll obviously have to palm them off onto my collector, who I doubt will be interested in any more books of poetry. So what the fuck would I want with them?'

'Hey, we had a deal! Two hundred and seventy-five bucks! You can't pull out now.'

'Really? Did I sign something, Sinclair?'

'What? No, you can't—'

Jack hung up the phone. *Fuck*. Before speaking to Chester, he had believed there was a slim possibility the police might leave him alone. Not anymore.

He needed to buy a couple of newspapers, see if anything had been written up about Kass's death. Jack slipped on his jacket, wound on his scarf and left the shop. There was a newsagent up the road.

He had just got back and was scanning the front page of one of the newspapers at the counter when Detective Peterson and Detective Sergeant Glendenning walked in. Peterson was grinning, arms casually slung into the pant pockets of his dark blue suit. Jack could hear keys jingling as he approached the counter. Glendenning followed: olive-green jacket and black pants, head down, stern faced, throwing quick sideways glances along the aisles of books. His shoes squeaked, but not like leather. Jack had known in his waters that the day was going to start with their arrival, no matter what time that was. He had been hoping for later.

'These old books, they really stink, don't they? How do you stand it all day?' Peterson grimaced and puffed out his chest. 'Like being locked up in an old woman's closet.'

'Wouldn't know,' said Jack. 'Never been in one myself.'

Peterson's brow tightened over his eyes like a belt. Jack casually flipped though the paper.

'Good morning,' said Glendenning. Nothing in his tone told Jack a thing. The detective moved up and stood beside Peterson, looking over the counter, itemising everything there with his steely cop eyes. 'Sleep well?'

'Not bad. Yourself?'

'Fine, thank you.'

'Good.'

Silence, except for the rumble of buses on York Street. Jack waited, pretending to read. Nobody said anything. Glendenning was obviously a fan of awkward pauses. He was working the room.

Peterson broke the spell. 'How's Chester?' Jack looked up. He noticed Detective Sergeant Glendenning's shoulders flinch, the barest movement, like he was annoyed. Peterson cleared his throat. 'Seen him lately?'

'No,' replied Jack. He wondered who held the superior rank between the two. Glendenning looked around, as though he was bored. Jack got the impression the two detectives were not best friends: or maybe he just hoped that was the case.

Glendenning nodded at the newspapers. 'What's new?'

'Everything's too expensive and the crime rate's up.'

'Same old thing,' said Peterson with a sneer. 'Living in the city was always shit.' He eyed Jack like he wanted to twist his arm. 'Unless you're your own boss, run your own business. With a little on the side now and then.'

Jack grinned, but not too much. 'I was thinking about joining you guys,' he said. 'High crime rate equals good job security. Plus the little extra on the side now and then.'

Peterson threw Jack a look like a back-handed slap. 'Pity reading books doesn't count as a qualification.' His pale face looked gaunt under the dull fluorescent light. With his blonde hair and frosty eyes and snarling contempt he would have made a perfect Nazi.

'You got a crime section?' asked Detective Sergeant Glendenning.

Jack nodded.

'Read much yourself?'

'More of late.'

'Courtroom drama or police procedural?'

'Psychological thrillers,' said Jack.

Glendenning nodded and looked around. 'I like the police procedural.'

'Maybe you should start writing your own.'

'Yeah, I've thought about that.' The detective locked his eyes on Jack but spoke to Peterson. 'What do you think, Geoff? I could write this one up.'

Peterson smiled. He had a big ugly mouth with loose rubber-band lips. 'Plenty of twists and turns.'

'I could do you a nice deal on a dictionary and a thesaurus,' said Jack. He looked the two detectives up and down. 'Throw in a style guide, too.'

Detective Glendenning put a hand in his pocket. Jack noticed it bulge with a fist. Maybe his mobile phone was in there. Or maybe it was an anger-management technique.

'Why don't *you* write it for us?' said Glendenning. It did not sound like a question. 'You know more than we do.'

'About what?'

Glendenning shrugged, looked away. 'Oh, about lots of things, I'm sure.'

Jack rubbed his hands together, softly cracked a couple of knuckles. The cops watched him. He looked around. He was starting to feel like a nine-year-old altar boy who needed to go to the toilet.

Peterson leaned on the counter. 'Come on, don't play the dumb fuck.'

'That's a good first line for your book.'

'Would you rather we dragged your arse down to the station?'

'Just watch the clichés.'

Detective Peterson turned to Glendenning. 'Not cooperating with an official police investigation.'

'Technically obstructing.' Glendenning stared blankly at Jack.

'Technically giving me the shits.' Peterson scowled.

'Am I supposed to read your minds?' said Jack. 'So far you haven't even told me why you're here.'

Detective Sergeant Glendenning rubbed the faint blue stubble on his chin. 'We know somebody is paying you to find some Edward Kass books,' he said. 'We'd like to know who that is.'

Jack realised he had been clenching his stomach. It loosened a little. They were not here about the other guy. They were following up angles. Connections. But it was only half a relief. Jack was not sure it was in his interests to tell them anything about Hammond Kasprowicz. He thought about the burnt books and Celia Mitten and the typewriter in Kasprowicz's study. He thought about Ian Durst. He thought about Annabelle Kasprowicz. Was he trying to protect her or himself? He was not sure what to think. Jack remembered Ziggy Brandt in the back of the big black Benz one day, spread out like he was on a banana lounge, handing out advice to a concerned gentleman who seemed to have some kind of problem. The guy called Ziggy, *Mr Brandt*. He had little beads of sweat on his forehead. Ziggy told him: 'If you've got nothing to give, always keep your mouth shut with the coppers. Always.' Jack remembered the big black Benz and the gold Rolex and the Armani suits. Maybe sometimes Mr Brandt knew what he was talking about.

'Chester Sinclair is full of shit,' said Jack. 'Four-year-olds know more than he does.'

'Please don't waste our time, Mr Susko.'

'I work for myself. That's why my name's on the sign outside.'

Peterson looked at Glendenning. He pushed himself off the counter, stood up straight. 'He wants to be difficult.'

Detective Sergeant Glendenning turned and walked around in a small circle, looking down at his shoes. 'No, I'm sure Mr Susko wants to help us to the best of his abilities.' He ran a finger along a bookshelf and then rolled the dust against his thumb. 'There's no reason to be difficult. Not any I can see.'

Glendenning walked back over, hands in his pockets. Unlike Peterson, he had the face of a man with huge reserves of patience, like some kind of police Zen master. *Time is on my side because I am time.*

'I had a lot of enquiries about Kass,' said Jack, clearing the newspapers from the counter. 'School kids, mainly. I thought maybe he'd been selected for a high school English list. Then I found out he was no longer in print. Thought I might corner the market.'

Peterson laughed. 'We got ourselves an entrepreneur!'

'Yeah, another hundred thousand and I've cracked my first mill. If you guys ever need a loan.'

Glendenning eyed Jack like he was looking through a gun sight. 'So you're not working for any collector?'

'No.'

Detective Sergeant Glendenning nodded, though not necessarily because he believed what he heard.

'Funny that Kass was sitting at the kitchen table when he was shot. Just doing his work like that,' said Jack.

'Why?' asked Peterson. His eyes flashed a little. Glendenning's stayed blank.

'Well, he obviously didn't hear the intruder break in.'

The two detectives said nothing.

'Implies the intruder snuck up on him.' Jack pushed his point. 'Shooting a man in the head that didn't even know you were there is a pretty dramatic turn for a simple break and enter. Don't you think?'

Now Peterson smirked, as though Jack had no idea what he was talking about. Glendenning breathed through his nostrils, slowly, and took his time blinking, as though he was holding a good hand but was unsure how much to bet.

Jack went on: 'Broke in, tiptoed into the kitchen, found Kass wondering if his last two lines should rhyme and just let rip. Bang.'

A look slipped between the two cops like a whisper. A moment later, Peterson leaned an elbow against the counter and turned towards his partner. Whatever his eyes said had no impact on Glendenning's poker face.

Jack moved the chair over from in front of his desk and leaned against the back of it. 'Had he stolen anything? Did he leave his prints anywhere else in the house, looking for something of value?'

'I thought it was psychological thrillers, Mr Susko.' Glendenning's voice was a monotone, but each word was tied to a lead sinker.

'I forgot to mention the odd Maigret.'

'What the hell's that?' asked Peterson, turning his head slightly in Jack's direction. Nobody answered him.

'I didn't notice anything in the killer's possession. No bag lying around anywhere,' said Jack. 'Everything in the living area looked untouched, the bedroom, too. Unless, of course, Kass worked for a terrorist organisation and there was a piece of paper with a secret code that could wreak havoc on the Dow Jones index slipped inside the intruder's Nike track pants.'

Glendenning looked away, down an aisle of books. 'Maybe there was. What else do you think, Mr Susko?'

'You're the experts.' But ideas were starting to pop into Jack's head. 'Was there much time between Kass's shooting and Durst's arrival?'

Glendenning did not turn back. 'Why?'

'Because if there was—'

The front door swung open and a customer walked into Susko Books. Jack pulled himself up and smiled hello. He remembered where he was. It occurred to him that he was talking too much. Thinking out aloud. Not a very good idea.

The customer headed to a display of art books across from the counter.

'Anything else, Maigret?' Glendenning asked.

'You going to put me on the payroll?'

'Maybe we just won't put you in jail.'

'For helping you solve a crime?' Jack smiled.

Peterson stood up and turned around. 'For talking shit,' he said.

'That's your speciality, Geoff.'

'You got a smart mouth.' Detective Geoff Peterson squared up. He had a couple of inches on Jack and used them for emphasis. 'How about I teach it some manners?'

'How about an official complaint?'

'Let me help you with the paperwork. I'll make sure it goes to the front of the queue.'

Detective Sergeant Glendenning walked over and touched Peterson lightly on the arm. His partner's shoulders dropped about two millimetres but his face still looked hard and mean. Obergruppenführer Peterson.

'You are aware that this is a murder investigation, Mr Susko?' said Glendenning. 'I'd hate there to be any confusion.'

'Perfectly clear.'

Jack wondered if he had gone too far. He was not sure what he was doing, but pissing the cops off was not what he wanted. It seemed he possessed a raw talent for it. Maybe from now on he would start not wanting things that he actually did want. Maybe he would start with not wanting an Aston Martin DB9 with a full tank and a long open road leading the hell out of there.

Glendenning's mobile phone began to ring. He put it to his ear. 'Fine. We're five minutes away.' The detective turned to go. 'We'll continue our conversation later,

Mr Susko.' His voice was low but firm. 'I'll call you tomorrow.'

'I'll be in and out for most of the day.'

'That's all right. We're a twenty-four-hour service.' Glendenning paused at the front door and turned back to Jack. 'Edward Kass was dead only minutes before Durst got there,' he said.

'What time was that?'

Glendenning narrowed his eyes. 'We're not exactly sure. Why, did you hear something?'

Jack hesitated. 'No.'

'You're still thinking, Mr Susko,' said the Detective Sergeant. Then he smiled. 'Tell me.'

'Nothing to tell.'

'But plenty to think about, eh? We'll have a nice chat tomorrow.'

Peterson and Glendenning left. The customer over by the art books looked up. Jack did not mean to frown at him, but did, and the man returned his attention to the book in his hands. Jack rubbed his forehead. It was only 10.20 a.m.

~16~

An hour later, Brendan MacAllister phoned. 'Jackie! How's my favourite lazy bastard?'

'Busy.'

'You poor man. Feel like a short break in the country?'

'Do I have to travel with you?'

'You can ride in the boot!' MacAllister laughed. 'I'm going down to Bowral tomorrow morning to see Clifford Harris.'

'The telecommunications guy?'

'Home loans.'

Jack remembered. 'Mister one hundred million in the bank. Loves coffee-table books with lots of female nudes.'

'He's off to Tuscany, bought a vineyard or village or

something, the prick. He rang yesterday and offered me first pickings of his book collection.'

'Nice.'

'I sold him most of it, but there's only a couple of things I'm interested in. Thought of you for the rest.'

'Sounds great. I'll just leave a sign here saying: *Help yourself, leave money on the counter.*'

'It's okay, I've spoken to Denise. She'll come in for you until we get back.'

'You sure?'

'Yeah, it's fine. She misses our old shop.'

'This isn't quite the same thing.'

'Don't worry about it. What do you say? He's a gourmet snob so there'll be brunch.'

Jack thought of his new detective friends. 'What time?'

'I'll pick you up at eight.'

'Say thanks to Denise for me.'

MacAllister scoffed. 'She's started some new diet. There's nothing to eat in the house except rice biscuits and low-fat yoghurt.'

'I can't believe you're not in hospital.'

'I told her I'm moving back in with my mother if she doesn't quit by Monday.'

'Make sure you give me the new number.'

MacAllister grunted. 'I've got to go. The plumber's here flashing his crack all over the bathroom and charging me for the view.'

'See you tomorrow.'

'Eight. Be ready.' MacAllister began singing *Oh Jackie Boy, the books, the books are calling* and hung up the phone.

Jack felt a sense of relief and was a little surprised by it.

Was he more worried about the cops than he was willing to admit?

In the morning, traffic kept them within the city limits for over an hour. Parramatta Road was a nightmare. Busy swearing, MacAllister missed the turn onto the Hume Highway and had to wind slowly through a selection of low-slung, rain-wet suburbs until he found it again. The scenic route: potholed roads, greasy front yards grey with exhaust fumes, and droopy awnings over the shops. Time took its time around here. Rent was cheap and so were the businesses: hot chips and chicken rolls, Halal butchers, Vietnamese grocers, Macedonian accountants with bilingual signs. Jets flew regularly overhead, low enough to hit with a tennis ball. People were either stuck in their cars, on the trains, or unemployed. Go West, Young Man!

Traffic loosened up a little once they were on the highway, but MacAllister still strained along at seventy kilometres an hour. His car of choice was a white, 1988 automatic Volvo. In terms of distance, it had been around the world two hundred times and probably had one more noisy lap in it. In terms of style, it was always going nowhere at Mach 2.

It began to rain again. The water on the road peeled off the tyres like glue, curling in small perfect waves.

'See the paper this morning?' said MacAllister. His tone was cool, on the serious side. He nodded towards the back seat. 'Take a look. Page three.'

Jack stretched around for a copy of the *Daily Telegraph*. He knew what it was going to be about even before he picked it up.

Poet shot in home invasion

by John Ecclestone

AN ACCLAIMED POET was shot dead in his Potts Point apartment yesterday after an attempted burglary, say local police. Edward Kass, 72, was found slumped over his kitchen table at approximately 4.30 p.m. with a bullet wound to the head. The intruder, whose name has not been released by police, was also found dead at the scene. Ian Douglas Durst, 43, arrived at the Kass apartment during the attempted burglary and surprised the intruder, wherein a struggle ensued and another shot was fired, fatally wounding the gunman. The murdered poet's daughter, Ms Celia Mitten, 46, arrived home with a friend soon after and discovered the gruesome scene.

Police held Mr Durst for questioning but released him a short time later. No charges have been laid. Last year, Mr Durst, a former gynaecologist, was involved in a drug and insider-trading scandal that saw him struck from the medical register.

Edward Kass was the recipient of numerous literary awards for his poetry. His brother, well-known Sydney business entrepreneur Hammond Kasprowicz, was unavailable for comment yesterday.

Jack folded the newspaper and tossed it onto the rear seat.

'Did you know?' asked MacAllister.

'I was there.'

'What?'

'I'm the friend. I walked in with Celia Mitten.'

'Jesus. What were you doing there?'

'Meeting Kass.'

'Why?'

'To get some ideas. Celia came to the shop a few days ago and told me somebody had burnt her father's books and sent them to him in the mail. A note said more would follow. Something like *and soon it'll be as if you never wrote any books at all*.'

'Christ.'

'I've seen the note but not the ashes.'

MacAllister thought for a moment. 'And you're getting hold of the same books for Kasprowicz?'

'You got it. She thinks it's him.'

'Have you asked Kasprowicz about it?'

'He denies it, says I'm crazy, but won't tell me why he wants them.'

'What do you think?'

'Not sure. But even his own daughter wouldn't put it past him. Apparently Kass didn't mind a bit of Mrs Kasprowicz on the side, once upon a time. I suppose that kind of thing can put a strain on sibling relations.'

'Jesus, these people! You don't know who's paying and who's drinking!'

'I'm sure there's something else, something I don't know. Why would he suddenly decide to burn his brother's books for something that happened so long ago?'

MacAllister shrugged his shoulders. 'Maybe he's one of those guys who bottles things up.'

Jack shook his head. 'Kasprowicz had already taken his brother to the cleaners over the family money, you told me that. And that was years ago. I was hoping Kass was going to give me a hint about where things stood with rich brother Hammond now.'

Roadwork machinery stood abandoned beside the highway, parked unevenly near newly laid asphalt and between large sections of concrete pipe. Loose gravel bounced up into the wheel arches.

MacAllister slowed and leaned forward in his seat, concentrating like a pensioner. 'You think the shooting's got something to do with the whole book burning thing?'

'Maybe.'

'I don't know,' said MacAllister, doubtfully. 'This is a big city. All sorts of things happen.'

Jack stretched a little in his seat, felt an itchiness around his stitches. He wondered if he should tell MacAllister. 'Yeah, but think about it. Kass was at the kitchen table working on his couplets when he got it in the head. From behind. Then Durst is suddenly there and he shoots the killer almost immediately after Kass gets it. Sound like a burglary gone terribly wrong?'

'I've heard stranger things.' MacAllister watched a car pass them. 'What did the police say?'

'Nothing. They're too busy following wrong leads.'

'What do you mean?'

Jack sucked in a deep breath. 'One of the detectives found out I used to work for Ziggy Brandt.' It was a touchy subject: he had left MacAllister's to work for Brandt.

'I told you not to take that fucking job!'

'Doesn't matter now.'

'It always matters with the cops.' MacAllister rubbed his beard vigorously. 'Always will. Permanently on the books now. I told you that. Suspicious by association.'

'Not that old record. You're worse than the fucking cops.'

Jack had not meant it to sound like that. He loved the guy, but the truth was different engines drove them. MacAllister stuck to the straight line and Jack liked to change lanes.

'How old are you?' MacAllister frowned. 'Fifteen?'

Jack ignored him.

'Don't be an idiot. The police are probably talking to Kasprowicz about the burnt books right now. Then they'll be back to talk to you again 'cause they'll want to know why you withheld stuff. Why, what, when, over and over, because they won't believe anything you say until you've said it fifty times. And then they'll arrest you for being a smart-arse. Just like last time. You already know the drill.'

'Yeah, I know it.'

Brendan MacAllister raised his voice. 'Why the hell did you have to visit Kass? What's it got to do with you if Kasprowicz is burning the books? The whole thing is none of your business. Soon as you found out you should have quit. Kasprowicz probably *is* burning the fucking books!'

Jack stared out of the window.

MacAllister glanced at him. 'Listen, you might want to start using that grey pulpy shit in your head. Don't get involved with these people. No matter what you think, you've got no idea what's going on. Like you said, Durst was at the fucking apartment and shot the guy. He was probably there because he's fucking Kass's daughter. Who knows what else? And what if the shooting wasn't a coincidence, like you said? All the possible scenarios look crap to me.' MacAllister eased off the accelerator a little. 'They live in another world, Jack. You should know that after working for Ziggy Brandt. I'm not helping you out of another fucking mess.'

Jack pulled out a cigarette and played with it. Outside, cars streamed through heavier rain—their rear lights blurred and dimmed, then were swallowed by the downpour.

'The guy who shot Kass was the same guy who stabbed me.'

MacAllister grimaced as though somebody had twisted his arm.

'Last Monday night somebody broke into the shop,' continued Jack. 'I walked in on the guy and he pulled a knife. Same guy. Not bad, huh?'

'Jesus.'

'He tried to light a little bonfire of Kass's books in my rubbish bin.'

MacAllister gripped the steering wheel tighter. 'What did the cops say when you told them?'

'I didn't tell them.'

'Why?'

'I want to find out who the fuck is trying to set me up.'

'Don't you think the cops would be better at that?'

Jack paused. 'I'm seeing Annabelle Kasprowicz.'

'Oh, for Christ's sake!'

'Calm down or you'll drive us off the road.' Jack wiped at his foggy window with a sleeve, the unlit cigarette in his fingertips. 'I want to keep seeing her.'

'Okay, no more,' said MacAllister, shaking his head. 'Don't tell me any fucking more, I don't want to know about it.'

'Whatever you say.'

'Yep, that's what I say. Enough.' MacAllister straightened up behind the wheel. 'Soon you'll be having a fucking *menage à trois* with Durst. Or maybe you already are? A big, all-in fuck festival at the Kasprowicz house!'

'Every Saturday night.'

'Yep, every Saturday night. I should have guessed.'

MacAllister leaned into the windscreen. Jack sank into his seat. The windows began to fog with their brooding.

They stopped to piss at a roadside truck stop, holding their breath against the stench of the chemical toilets. They drove on. Here and there a smoky mist lay through clusters of trees and hovered over low corners of the paddocks around them. Even with the drenching, the land looked brown and useless.

Half an hour later they turned off the Hume and drove through the town of Mittagong. The sky was still bloated with clouds. The place was almost empty. Jack saw a skinny woman with stringy blonde hair, smoking a cigarette under the post-office awning and ignoring the toddler crying into her leg. She looked up as they drove past. Her face was too long for so early in the day.

'How far to Clifford's place?' asked Jack. He wound the window down to let a little air in.

'Not far.'

A few kilometres later, the town of Bowral. Half-a-dozen more and they turned left onto a narrow sealed road, edged with gravel and shallow muddy gutters. Then another forty minutes with not much to see but a lot of silent land getting wet.

Eventually they drove into a stand of eucalyptus trees and tall pines and what looked like cedar, black with rain. Waist-high bushes and ferns, swaying in the wind. The car rumbled over a small timber bridge with a creek rushing underneath. They passed a gatehouse and drove under a thin metal arch with creepers twisted around it. There were letters welded there, too. They spelled *Kininmonth* in long curly script. Jack looked at MacAllister.

'It means *rich bastard*.'

They came into the open again and followed a curved carriage driveway up a gentle rise. Gravel crunched pleasantly as they came over the low hill. Kininmonth. After the Great Wall of China, it was probably the next thing you could see from the moon.

'Jesus,' said Jack. 'Monarch of the fucking Glen.'

The driveway bisected perfect lawns, rows of white and yellow rose bushes, and thick green hedges at least ten feet high. The house was grey granite, streaked with rain. Gabled roofs, crow-stepped and castellated parapets, and six chimney stacks in case it got cold during a siege. Jack could only imagine how many rooms it had. There was probably a spare ballroom somewhere to keep the dustpan and broom in.

They got out of the car. MacAllister heaved a doorknocker the size of a church bell. They waited in the vaulted alcove, looking around. After a while, the front door opened.

MacAllister smiled broadly. 'Morning, Mr Harris.'

Clifford Harris looked fifty, with longish straw-blonde hair and not-quite-ironed-out wrinkles around his eyes. He was tall and paunchy, no chin, small grey eyes and a buttery complexion. Whatever he had that might have appealed to women was mostly in his wallet. He was wearing jeans, polished black leather boots and a tight white shirt with military style lapels. There was a silver watch on his wrist that was probably no good for his posture. He seemed annoyed.

'Brendan. I wasn't expecting you until the afternoon.'

MacAllister gave him a perplexed look. 'I thought you said any time was fine?'

'It doesn't matter now.' Clifford Harris turned to Jack.

'This is Jack Susko,' said MacAllister. 'He works for me.'

Harris nodded but did not offer his hand. 'Fine.' He walked back into the house. 'Wipe your shoes.'

Jack had a strong feeling that no brunch would be forthcoming.

The entrance foyer echoed with their footsteps. It was about the size of a Masonic hall. The walls were covered in wood-and-gilt-framed paintings of plump, naked nymphs lying around pools of crystal water in the forest, or reclined on luxurious floor cushions with Negro attendants offering ripe fruit in baskets. Plants rested on elaborate steel stands. Large, empty vases and an array of chairs too valuable to sit on posed here and there against the walls, some tables and sideboards between them. There was a gold-edged mirror, big enough for twenty people to look at themselves — or for one person to be the centre of a lot of their own attention.

Harris led them down a wide hallway of smooth pale stone under a patterned maroon runner. After about a hundred metres he stopped. 'In there,' he said, pointing. They walked into a long rectangular room with high ceilings and a window at one end covered with drawn white blinds. There was a parquet floor, a couple of armchairs, some lamps and a small purple-upholstered couch. The bookshelves were painted white.

'Can you be quick?' said Harris. 'I have guests.'

'No problem,' replied MacAllister, already scanning the shelves. 'We'll leave the keys in the letterbox.'

Harris frowned. He placed a hand on one of the bookshelves. He had a vaguely effeminate manner. Jack wondered if maybe his aunts had raised him.

MacAllister angled his head and squinted at the book spines. Halfway along the shelf he stopped, pulled out one of the books and inspected it. He glanced over at Jack. 'I didn't know you collected poetry, Mr Harris.'

Clifford squinted at the book in MacAllister's hands. 'I don't. That was a gift from a friend. He knew the poet.'

'Not for sale, then?'

'Oh no. It's for sale. It's all for sale.'

Jack walked over and MacAllister passed him the book. A slim, brown leather volume with gilt stamping. He flipped to the cover plate. *Selected Poems*. Privately bound. Signed and numbered by the author. This was number three. The author was Edward Kass.

MacAllister ran his eyes over a few more spines. 'Looks like a complete collection.'

Harris half shrugged, half nodded, as if to say *of course*. 'I've never looked at them,' he said nonchalantly.

'Don't tell your friend,' said Jack. 'He might get offended.'

Clifford Harris scoffed. 'He wouldn't mind at all. You can ask him if you like, he's one of my guests. Doctor Ian Durst.'

Jack's head snapped up.

Harris noticed the look on his face. 'Do you know him?'

It took a couple of pulses of Jack's synapses for the

information to fully register in his brain. He frowned with the effort. Then his head started to hurt.

Clifford Harris repeated the question. 'Do you know him?'

Jack pulled himself together. 'I know he's not a doctor anymore.'

Harris passed a soft, pink hand across his fringe of soft, dyed hair. His voice was tight with offence. 'Then you don't know a thing. And I'd prefer you leave gossip and lies outside where you wiped your feet.'

Jack grinned.

Harris puffed himself up, indignant, as though a valet had put a scratch in his Range Rover. 'I've known Ian for fifteen years,' he said, raising his voice. 'What the media did to that man's life is an absolute disgrace.' His doughy cheeks glowed pink for a moment. 'My wife still sees him regularly,' he added in a defiant tone.

'No, you're right, it was terrible.' Jack tuned a little flattery into his voice. 'So you'd know the Kasprowicz family, too?'

'Of course. I first met Ian through his father-in-law, Hammond Kasprowicz. He was a business partner of mine.'

Jack nodded, pursing his lips slightly, his face a polite, standard *Oh right, yes I see* kind of face. What he was thinking was how beautifully neat everything was. How unbelievable, even. Durst was here? Now? What surprised Jack, though, was that he was not surprised at all.

'So you knew the brother, Edward?'

'I only ever met him once. Many years ago. We exchanged pleasantries.'

Jack watched Harris' face closely. Clifford shifted his eyes for an instant to MacAllister and then cleared his throat. 'I suppose you've heard?' he said. 'He was murdered two days ago. Horrible news.'

'Shocking,' said Jack. He held up the book in his hands. 'Anybody ever approached you about these, offering to buy?'

Harris seemed uncomfortable for a moment. But then it passed and he went back to exuding his effeminate arrogance. 'As a matter of fact, yes. Hammond Kasprowicz made an offer on them only a few weeks ago.'

It was getting better by the minute. 'But you said no?'

'I'd rather lose a testicle than help Hammond Kasprowicz in any way whatsoever.'

'Your business together didn't go too well?'

'He's a cunt.'

'Seems a popular opinion.'

Harris moved towards the door of the library. 'Even his daughter thinks so.'

Jack felt a little sting. 'Do you know her?'

'Annabelle? Well, of course. She's Ian's *wife*.'

Jack felt another sting. It took its time passing. 'Aren't they divorced?'

Harris smirked. 'Appearances are necessary sometimes,' he replied, preening. He pointed his little chin and stretched the wrinkles in his creamy neck. He obviously enjoyed knowing things. 'Let's just say there are certain legal technicalities that need to be taken care of. And I am assisting. Everybody needs help against pricks like Kasprowicz.'

Jack lowered his eyes for a moment. Thoughts were coming fast now. Unpleasant ones.

'I'll leave you to it.' Harris headed for the door. 'Be quick.'

MacAllister stood for a moment, listening to Clifford Harris' footsteps fade away down the hall. Then he turned around. He placed his big hairy hands on his hips and pointed his big hairy chin at Jack. His big placating grin was gone. 'So what do you think now?' he said, in an angry whisper.

'What's there to think?'

MacAllister blew a hard breath through his nostrils. 'Yeah, that's it, you're right. There's nothing to think. Nothing at all. Because you already know everything.'

Jack turned away. He had had enough.

'You're the smartest bastard in the world.'

'That's right,' said Jack through his teeth. 'Uncle Brendan.'

He walked out of the library and down the hall. Outside he leaned against the wall of the front-door alcove and breathed in the cold wet air. He lit a cigarette and tried not to think about Annabelle Kasprowicz.

Which proved difficult. She was walking directly towards him.

~17~

SHE WORE ALL THE RIGHT GEAR for a morning gallop: tight black boots, biscuit-brown jodhpurs, a thick high-necked white jumper and a powder-red raincoat. A belt hung loosely around the buttoned waist. She carried a black riding helmet in her right hand, a stiff black riding crop in the other. Her hair was tied back, her cheeks flushed, her nose a little pinched and shiny. Country morning fresh. The stable boys must have fallen over themselves to help her into the saddle.

Jack watched her face: if she was surprised to see him, only she knew about it. There was a slight hesitation in her stride as she looked up at the house and scanned the windows, but she kept on coming. Then she was standing in front of him, keeping the one step up into the alcove between them.

'Nice ride?' asked Jack.

'What are you doing here?'

'Working. You?'

She looked over his shoulder into the house. 'It's not how it looks.'

'You haven't seen the view from here.'

'We brought Louisa down to stay. Our house is under siege from reporters. She doesn't need the drama.'

Jack nodded, smoked. He flicked ash from the cigarette. 'These country millionaires come in handy sometimes.'

'Don't be like that. My father isn't back yet and we ... I ...'

'It must be great for your daughter to see her parents cooperating so well. Putting her first. I mean, with the divorce and everything.'

Annabelle turned away.

Jack looked at the side of her face, taking in every detail. All he could confirm was that she was beautiful. 'Comfortable night?' he asked.

'Shall I show you where I slept?'

'It's still early. No need to disturb anyone.'

'You're a prick.'

'When I'm in the mood.'

Annabelle stepped up into the alcove and went to walk past him.

Jack grabbed her by the arm and pulled her close. 'You want to tell me what the fuck's going on?'

'I just told you.' She tried to shake her arm free. 'Let go of me!'

He released her. Her eyes were hard and unfriendly and Jack had the feeling that everything between them had just evaporated. Maybe there had been nothing to begin with.

He turned away and threw his cigarette to the ground. He looked out over the smooth billiard-felt lawns and into the tall wet trees along the stone-walled boundary, and up the slope at the smoky horizon. Maybe what he needed to do was go for a long walk. Clear his head. A hundred miles ought to do it.

'Jack.' Annabelle was still standing behind him. 'Please.' Her voice was softer now, a tone of helplessness at its edges. 'You have to understand. Louisa is having a rough time and now all this has happened, too. My father's away and I'm in the house alone. I don't have that many options.'

'I'd say you had more than one.' Jack kept his back to her, waited. Nobody moved, nobody spoke.

'Jesus, you think I *want* to be here?'

Jack turned around, slowly. 'You telling me you can't afford a hotel?' he said, feeling heat rise up his back. 'Or a quick trip to New York, Hong Kong, London, Paris, wherever the fuck you want?'

She gave him a look of contempt. 'It's not that simple.'

'Yeah, right. All that bank balance but not five cents' worth of imagination.' He shook his head. 'It's bullshit.'

'Oh, if only you were rich, if only you had money!' Annabelle sneered. 'There'd be nothing to worry about, would there? No problems, no dramas, everything would be perfect all the time. God, you'd be so fucking good at it, wouldn't you, Jack?'

'That's not what I'm talking about.'

'Yeah, right.' Annabelle lowered her voice. 'Everything

I've got can be taken away from me. Do you understand? Louisa. Money. My whole future. You think it's easy for me?'

'Must be terrible. Did the horse ride help?'

'Fuck you! What the hell do you know about any of it?'

'I know a load of crap when I hear it.'

Annabelle threw her helmet at him.

Jack moved to his left and caught it. He grinned, turned the helmet over in his hands a few times and then put it on his head. It was a couple of sizes too small. 'What about the whip?'

Annabelle came up and pushed him hard in the chest. The helmet fell off and rolled down the step, out onto the driveway gravel.

'You think you know everything, don't you?' she said, holding the whip down by her leg like a knife. 'I'm just the sad, little rich girl with too much money and time and nothing to do?' She moved in closer and hissed at him. 'Nothing to do but fuck good-looking bastards like you?'

'Thanks for the compliment.'

She pushed him again.

'Hey, I'm just after a straight answer,' he said, frowning. 'All you keep giving me is right angles.'

'Straight answer to what? I'm stuck between a bad mistake that won't go away and a twisted old bastard that happens to be my father. Neither of them gives a shit about me and both of them can take it all away. Straight enough for you?'

'So what do you want from me?' said Jack. 'Pick you up and ride you out to my castle?'

'Your castle?' Annabelle Kasprowicz laughed. A hard,

nasty laugh. Jack flushed a hot shade. Women always knew where to aim the high heel.

He grabbed her wrist. It was soft and thin and the thought flashed through his mind that he could snap it like a matchstick. He eased his grip. Annabelle let her shoulders sag and Jack sensed her body relinquishing. He brought his other hand up and took hold of her chin. He pushed her head back a little and turned it to the side, like he was inspecting it for flaws. She let him. She was flawless. A tear slipped down over her perfect cheekbone. Jack watched it reach his finger.

He had not heard the approaching footsteps.

'Get the fuck away from my wife.'

Annabelle made a noise but swallowed it. Jack let go of her and looked up. Durst had come through the front door, holding a shotgun. He held it with a certain professional nonchalance, like a butler might hold a towel on his arm for the Duke of Gloucester. The butt was tucked under his elbow and the smooth black, under-and-over barrels stretched out across his forearm, open.

Durst snapped the gun shut. Jack had not had time to notice if it was loaded. The two dark cylinders pointed at his kneecaps. Suddenly they looked about a mile long.

'You're a son of a bitch,' said Durst. He lifted the shotgun a little higher and pointed it precisely at Jack's balls.

Clifford Harris walked out of the house and stood beside Durst, a double-barrel resting over his forearm, too. It looked more of an antique, the barrels side-by-side old style and engraved with Spanish-looking motifs, as was the stock and grip. He had been smiling as he walked out but when he saw Jack and Annabelle and then Durst, he stopped.

'What's going on?'

Durst and Harris wore identical, shiny brown leather vests with red and black cartridges slipped into ammunition sleeves cut into them—two sets of five over the chest, two more sets of five directly below. Between them they had enough to make a mess of a small family of woolly mammoths. Jack wondered if he should call out for MacAllister.

'That's the second gun I've seen you with in three days,' he said to Durst. 'You compensating for something?'

Annabelle moved towards him. 'Jack, don't.'

'Get the fuck inside,' snarled Durst at her. 'Go find your daughter.'

'Don't talk to me like that!' She spun around and advanced on Durst. The riding crop went up into the air. Durst grabbed her by the arm and pulled her aside. She stumbled and hit the alcove wall with her shoulder. Jack took a step forwards. Durst lifted the shotgun higher.

'Easy, lover boy.'

'You fuck!' cried Annabelle.

Clifford Harris put a hand on Durst's shoulder. 'Settle down. I think it's best if we just ask Mr Susko to be on his way.'

Durst's shotgun had moved slightly when he grabbed his ex-wife. Jack's balls were safe again. He took a quick step forward and swung a right at Durst's head: chin, cheek, eye, neck, anywhere was just fine. He connected mostly with ear, and a little with the area in front, where the jaw attaches to the skull. Fairy floss would be on the good doctor's menu until Christmas. Durst stumbled backwards. Jack moved with him; a second later his left came round at the end of a tight, right-angled jab and caught Durst square on the chin. It looked good, much prettier than the first punch. Durst's head snapped back again. The shotgun fell from his hands onto the flagstones. Annabelle yelled something and Harris moved at the edges of Jack's vision, but Jack only had eyes for Durst. He grabbed a handful of leather vest and pulled Durst forward, away from the wall and into some space. He let go with another right, straight into the guts: the money shot, the one Jack had been saving up since the first time they met. All the air in Durst's lungs blew out with a loud *ooohff*, like a gym mat being thrown to the floor. He went down and stayed down, curling up around his stomach and grimacing with pain.

Now they were even, with a little extra left over in the bank for Jack.

Somebody grabbed him from behind and pulled him backwards. They tried to pin his arms. Jack straightened up and threw his head back, hard as he could. He hit something bony and then heard a groan. His arms were no longer pinned. He turned around and saw MacAllister with his hands on his face.

'Jesus!' cried the big man as he doubled over. 'Fuck!'

Harris froze and stared at MacAllister. Jack moved quickly and snatched the shotgun out of his hands. Harris hardly seemed to notice.

'What'd you do that for?' said MacAllister, wincing. 'You've busted my fucking nose!' He stood up again and then looked at his hands. They were covered in blood. His nose was raw and swollen. He spat on the ground. 'Jesus!'

Annabelle went over to Jack and grabbed his arm. 'You should go.' She glanced down at Durst, still curled up on the flagstones, and then nodded at MacAllister. 'Go on, just go. Help him to your car.'

Jack leaned the shotgun on the wall behind him. His arms were very heavy. He could feel his heartbeat pound in his fists. He guided MacAllister to the Volvo and helped him into the passenger side. Then he got into the driver's seat. Annabelle waved him away and turned to Harris. They started to argue. Jack glanced up at Kininmonth and saw Annabelle's daughter, Louisa, staring down from one of the windows. He turned away and started the Volvo's engine. He tried to tell himself it was not always the bad guys that got driven out of town.

~*18*~

THE ADRENALINE FADED SLOWLY from Jack's body: his hands shook a little on the wheel. His guts were tight, shoulders stiff, the taste in his mouth metallic. Some light repartee might have helped, but MacAllister was not talking. He remained silent the whole way back to Sydney, even after Jack had stopped at a supermarket in Campbelltown and bought him a packet of frozen peas for his nose. Sometimes MacAllister had a tendency to sulk. This was one of them.

'What about a game of *I Spy*?'

MacAllister ignored Jack. He inspected the improvised cold pack and then switched on the radio. Classical music filled the car, along with a lot of static.

'Is that a no?' Jack glanced at his friend. A scowl flashed over MacAllister's face like a flame.

Eyes on the road and the rain, Jack drove and tried to remember to breathe. But his mind kept throwing punches, replaying the scene at Kininmonth, and his regret grew with every wet mile that slipped under the wheels.

At home, a couple of shots of Tullamore Dew did nothing to dispel the unease. Neither did a few more. Lois sensed the tension and stayed in the bedroom. Jack smoked and picked at the stitches in his stomach and thought about a lot of things that added up to nothing.

Slowly, silently, the afternoon soaked up the evening. He fell asleep on the couch.

Next thing, the phone rang. It was Annabelle Kasprowicz.

'I need to see you.'

Jack rubbed his face. 'What time is it?'

'Nearly midnight. I know it's late, but—'

'Where are you?'

'I'm at home. Please, can you come over?'

'What's the rush?'

'The police were here this afternoon. They rang me at Kininmonth and asked me to come back and answer some questions.'

'About what?'

'My father.' Annabelle paused. 'They think he had something to do with Edward's death.'

Jack tried to focus. The room was thick with darkness. He closed his eyes, lowered his head.

'And what did he have to say about it?'

'He didn't say anything. He's not here.'

'Isn't he back from Hong Kong?'

'No. And I don't know where he is. That's what they questioned me about. They think he never went to Hong Kong.'

Jack's mind started to sift a few things, but it was slow work at this time of night.

'He was meant to be back yesterday but I still can't get him on his mobile. I've been trying every five minutes since the police left. I'm afraid, Jack.'

Lois padded in from the bedroom. Jack leaned across and switched on the lamp. A soft reddish light spread through the lounge room. His arm twitched. He remembered Durst.

'Where's hubby?'

'Please, not now, Jack.'

The bottle of Tullamore Dew stood a third full on the coffee table. Jack poured himself a couple of fingers.

'I'm here alone,' said Annabelle. 'I can't sleep.'

'Too much hot-shoe shuffle.'

'What?'

'You heard.'

'*Jesus*, Jack.' Annabelle's voice tensed.

Jack slugged the whiskey. 'What was Clifford Harris talking about? Are you really getting a divorce or just playing a nice round of family swindle?'

'For God's sake! I've already told you. What do I need to say to make you believe me?'

'Try anything believable.'

'Okay. How's this? I'm glad you hit him. You loosened one of his teeth. He spent a lot of money on them.'

'His or your father's?'

'Mine.'

'I thought you didn't have any.'

'Not anymore.'

Jack turned his glass on the coffee table in small half-circles. 'So what's the deal? Who gets what in the society divorce of the year?'

'Goodnight, Jack. You know where I am.'

She hung up the phone.

Jack finished his drink and sat back in the couch. Lois climbed onto his lap. He reached for the stereo remote, turned the sound down a couple of notches and pressed play: Sarah Vaughan, smooth and warm and perfect.

If love is good to me.

Jack listened, eyes closed. Lois purred. *If love is good to me.*

A late bus came by on Oxford Street before Jack could hail an available taxi. He caught it to Bondi Junction and then jumped into a cab to Double Bay. He got out on the corner of New South Head Road and Bay Street. He wanted to walk, get some air.

Dark ragged clouds swept over a bright moon. Cars and buildings looked glassy with cold. Under the streetlights, fallen wet leaves like beached fish.

Bay Street was deserted. Jack walked and looked in the windows: a real-estate agent's, a couple of clothing stores and an antique shop with two huge terracotta pots shoulder to shoulder. One would have filled Jack's entire apartment. Then three shops in a row, all empty, with *For Lease* signs hung crookedly in their windows. Unopened mail strewn under the front doors. Jack noticed more of the same further on. *Closing Down Sale, 50% Off Everything, Last Days, End of Lease Bargains*. Looked like the Bay had seen better days.

It began to spit. He made it to Cumberland Gardens just as the drops fattened into rain. Annabelle saw him through a window and the front door was open before he had a chance to knock.

'Jack!' She hugged him and then stepped back. 'I'm so glad.'

'I charge eighty bucks an hour. Seventy-five for cash.' Jack smiled but he could see something was up. Her grip was tight on his hand.

'What's wrong?' he said.

Her eyes were tired, her face pale. Her hair looked a little slept-in, loose and messy. She was dressed casually in a long, moss green, belted mohair cardigan, a pair of jeans and suede moccasins. Jack thought she had never looked more beautiful.

'I have to show you something.'

'What?'

'I can't believe it, Jack. I just can't believe it.'

She closed the front door and led him down the hall, then left into another small corridor. They came to a pine door that had been sanded back but was yet to receive a coat of varnish. Annabelle opened it and flicked a light switch. Jack saw narrow stairs leading down below the house.

'The cellar,' said Annabelle.

She began to descend cautiously, side-saddle style, with one hand out against the wall. Jack followed, crouching a little beneath the low ceiling. He noticed the plaster walls had not been painted and the stairs were covered with footprints left in the plaster dust. Here and there, off-cuts of wiring and bits of timber and a few nails and screws. Jack wondered if the builder would ever be back to finish the renovation.

They reached the bottom. The air was cool and dull like paste, and smelt of dampness and wet dust. In the half-dark, Jack could see racks of wine running down either side of the rectangular room. The ceiling only cleared his head by a couple of inches. There must have been at least a thousand bottles of wine in there. And Jack doubted they were out of the bargain bin at the local liquor store.

Annabelle switched on another light. A bare globe with a metal cage around it jutted out from the middle of the ceiling. Jack thought of a torture room under a drug lord's mansion.

'Here,' said Annabelle. She handed him a small key and pointed at some metal lockers that lined the rear wall. There were six of them. 'Go and open one.'

'What have you got for me? A body?' As he said it, Jack realised that he was only half joking.

'Just look.'

Jack went to the lockers. He could not help but glance at the wine bottles in their racks—the labels on one row said *Penfold's Grange 1971*. Five hundred a pop, at least. Only quality hangovers for Hammond Kasprowicz.

He slipped the key into one of the middle lockers. It came open with a dull scrape of metal. Inside: books, boxes, framed photographs. Shoved in and packed tight. Jack turned and looked at Annabelle.

'Take out one of the books.'

Jack pulled out a slim volume: *The Cull* by Edward Kass. He leaned in and ran his eyes over the other spines. More copies of *The Cull*, plus some of *Entropy House*, and *Simply Even*. There were a lot of books. Enough to make Jack a little uncomfortable.

'So he stored them here,' he said. 'So what?'

'Look inside the boxes.'

He tugged at a shoebox, edged it out carefully and then lifted the lid. There were photographs in it. They had all been cut up into tiny pieces. It was like a box of confetti.

'There's more in the other lockers.' Annabelle's voice was hard, emotionless. 'They used to be photos of my mother.'

Jack put the box down and pulled out one of the framed photographs. The glass was broken, only a few splinters remained around the edges of the frame. Mrs Kasprowicz's face had been slashed and hacked, maybe with a pair of scissors. It was the same story with the other photos there. Those with Edward Kass in them had been given the same treatment.

'I know my father hated them both,' said Annabelle. 'But this?'

Jack turned to her. She was standing with her arms loose by her sides.

'There are burnt photos in other boxes. My mother had thousands of photos of herself. I remember going through them as a child. So many albums, envelopes stuffed with them. And he's destroyed them all.'

'He sure has.'

'Why would he keep them?'

'You'll have to ask him.'

She stared vacantly for a moment. 'You don't think he had anything to do with Edward's death?'

Jack thought of the cops. 'Doesn't matter what I think.' He walked over and gave Annabelle the key. 'How did you find this?'

'After I spoke to you I went into his study, hoping I'd find something that would tell me where he might be. I don't know, a receipt, a note, anything. In one of the bottom drawers of his desk I found a diary. The whole thing was blank, he hadn't written a word in it anywhere. Businesses send them to him all the time, he usually throws them out or gives them to Louisa. I didn't think there'd be anything there, but I flipped through it. The back cover slipped out of the leather sleeve of the jacket. The key was taped to it.'

Jack nodded. 'And here we are.' He thought of Edward Kass. He remembered the old man's dead body, flopped like a life-sized puppet over the kitchen table, blood dripping slowly down to the floor, thick, dull splashes onto that soaked tartan slipper.

Annabelle's moccasins scraped on the gritty concrete floor. 'What are you thinking?'

'Why would your old man just take off?' The stuff in the lockers had been there a long time.

'Maybe he panicked when he heard about Edward's death.'

Jack looked around the cellar. Hammond Kasprowicz was not the panicking type. 'Maybe.'

Annabelle put her hand on Jack's arm. 'Can you stay with me? I don't want to be alone when the police come.'

The cops were the last people Jack wanted to see. 'Sure.' The cellar was starting to make him feel claustrophobic. It was the middle of the night. It had already been an intense day. He should have been home in bed. Annabelle Kasprowicz had still not answered his question. 'I'll stay, but first tell me what's going on with Durst.'

'Are you serious? I'm asking for your help, Jack. Can't you drop it?'

'No.'

Tears glazed Annabelle's eyes. 'Fuck!'

'I want to help,' said Jack. 'But you have to tell me.'

'I thought maybe you loved me.'

'So what if I did?' Jack raised his voice. 'Why are you still screwing your ex-husband?'

'Don't.'

'Answer me.'

'I told you the story.'

'You're lying.'

'Fuck off.'

'No problem.' Jack made for the stairs.

'Wait!' Annabelle grabbed him by the arm. 'It's not what you think.'

'What is it then?'

She let go. Jack could see small red veins creeping into the corners of her eyes.

'Ian signed a pre-nup when we married,' she said, looking at Jack intently. 'All he gets is fifty thousand if we divorce. He owes a lot more than that.'

'So what? Sign the divorce papers and off you go.'

'It's not as simple as that.'

'Why?'

'Because if I do he'll take me to court. And if it goes to court, he'll ruin me.' Annabelle walked over to one of the wine racks, reached out with a hand and held on. She thought about something for a while. Then she said: 'I had an affair earlier in our marriage. He's got some tapes, some videos. I can't let them come out, Jack. Louisa would never speak to me again.'

'Who was it?' The question came out of Jack's mouth of its own accord.

'Nobody. It was nothing. But he was the father of Louisa's best friend. He's still with his wife. And his daughter is still Louisa's best friend.'

'So it's not about the money.'

'It is for Ian. And as far as my father's concerned. He can't understand why I won't sign the divorce papers. He wants Ian gone. Of course, he doesn't know about the tapes.'

'How did Durst get them?'

'Private investigator.' Annabelle wiped away some tears. 'Do you understand, Jack? Can you see?'

Above them a door slammed. Footsteps thudded down the hall. Annabelle looked at the ceiling and then rushed up the stairs. Jack took a deep breath. He looked over at the lockers for a moment and then followed, unhurried. The cops were going to love it. Hammond Kasprowicz was going to have a lot of explaining to do. So was Jack.

Annabelle met him at the top of the stairs. It was not her father who had arrived home.

'It's Louisa,' she said. 'You have to go.'

Jack nodded. 'You going to call the cops?'

'What choice have I got?'

'None.'

'Call me tomorrow.' Annabelle kissed him on the cheek and walked off down the corridor. She disappeared into the house.

As he left, Jack made as little noise as possible. He closed the front door with the barest click of the lock, and slipped away into the night. How was it that he found himself sneaking through the shadows once again?

~*19*~

At 7.45 the next morning, as Jack was about to head off to Susko Books, somebody knocked on his door. Something about the tone of the knock said: *Bad news*. Maybe he was just a little nervous. Hearing things that were not there. Maybe it was just a neighbour, over for a cup of sugar. He opened the door. Maybe not.

'They really should have a security system on the entrance here. Anybody can just walk in off the street. Bums, thieves, rapists.' Detective Geoff Peterson smiled. 'Stand-over guys wearing brass knuckles.'

He stood in the half-dark of the hall, smug and vaguely threatening. The light from Jack's apartment threw a shadow that sliced his tall sinewy body like a mayor's sash.

But he looked too shabby for the position. His hands were in his pockets. There were bags under his eyes. His tie was undone and the silvery-grey suit looked slept in. The face was pinched; the eyes loaded. And here was Jack, at point-blank range.

'Any light in here?' asked Peterson, looking down the entrance hall.

'All the bulbs were stolen. You looking for work?'

'What if somebody was waiting for you, hiding over there by the stairs? You open your front door, quick bang on the head, and they help themselves to the plasma TV.'

Lois miaowed in the lounge room. Peterson looked over Jack's shoulder and grinned. 'And then just for the hell of it they play with the cat and a box of matches.'

'Lucky we got you hanging around,' said Jack. 'Maybe we could get you a stool for the slow afternoon shift.'

'Might be someone with a gun or a knife. Up under the chin. *Inside motherfucker and keep it quiet!*'

'You know the lines, Detective. And the way it just rolled off your tongue. I almost forgot you were a cop.'

'They tie you up, ask politely where all the good stuff is. Then they kill the cat if you don't feel like talking.'

Jack tried to read Peterson's face but it was like a wet newspaper. Had Clifford Harris called the cops about his assault on Durst? Jack's guts told him no.

'*Hand over the cash you fuck!*' hissed the detective. His eyes were dry and red and a touch on the wired side.

'They'd get a haul, too,' said Jack. 'With all the cash I've got stashed in my socks and folded inside the hamburger buns in the freezer. Don't tell anyone.'

'He might have followed you to work, guessed that not

every dollar was declared to the tax department. These guys are smart cunts.'

'Smarter than you, Detective?' Jack began to close the door. 'I'll leave you to your hall monitoring.'

Peterson held his arm out and pushed the door open. A hard look of *I don't think so* flashed across his face. Jack stiffened, but then he eased off and played it cool. Getting hammered by the cops first thing in the morning was not on his list of things to do today.

He let go of the door and walked back into the apartment. He sat in the Eames chair, reached for a packet of cigarettes on the coffee table and lit up. He leaned back and watched Peterson close the front door.

'How's Hammond, Jack?'

So the cops knew he was working for the old man. Had Annabelle told them?

'That's the first thing we'll book you for: withholding information.'

'Okay,' said Jack.

'Should be able to squeeze out an accessory to assault there, too.'

'Sounds good.'

'You think I'm joking? We found his little collection, Susko. The one you helped get together. And we know all about the burnt books and the notes. That constitutes assault. Tell me, did Kasprowicz get you to light the matches as well?'

Outside the wind swirled dead acacia leaves around the courtyard. Jack turned and watched: maybe it was time he cleaned up out there. Sweeping was good honest work. Therapeutic, too.

'Didn't your mummy tell you playing with matches would get you into trouble?'

'You're just fishing, Detective,' said Jack. 'But there's nothing in the pond.'

'Talking the talk, eh? How about we add aiding and abetting the escape of a murder suspect?'

'Knock yourself out.'

'Kasprowicz didn't like that brother of his,' continued Peterson. 'Took him to the cleaners for the family money. Then he tried to fuck him with the burnt books. Then he just decided to do him in. And now he's done a runner.'

'Really? Where's he gone?'

'Nobody knows. Except maybe you.'

'Try Hong Kong.'

'We checked. They never saw him. Try again.'

'What about up your arse?'

The detective smiled. 'That's it, Jack. Dig the hole deeper. 'Cause you're going to get good and buried. I got the shovel in the car.'

'Sounds like it's personal, Detective. Did I fuck your sister or something?'

Peterson moved a little closer. Behind his back he flexed the fingers of his right hand. 'I know about the other guy at Kass's apartment, Jackie boy,' he said. There was cold steel in his tone. 'You know, the one who stabbed you the other day? The one who shot Kass in the head? The one you saw on the kitchen floor with a bullet in his chest? Good old Rory Champion. And that was his real name, too, in case you're wondering.'

Peterson let it all hang in the air for a moment. 'Not telling us about Rory was a bad move, Jack. Sounds a little like intent to pervert the course of an investigation. Or maybe it sounds a lot like it. So next we have to ask ourselves why. Don't we?'

Jack looked blankly at Peterson.

The detective grinned. ''Cause you're an accessory to murder, maybe?' he said, enjoying himself. 'People do all sorts of things for money.' Peterson looked around the apartment with distaste. 'And there's no doubt Kasprowicz could afford *you*.'

'I'm sure you can colour it any way you want, Detective. But it all looks bullshit brown to me.' Jack tried to sound smooth but it was all unsealed road from the moment he opened his mouth.

'Oh, I got all the colours of the rainbow right here.' Peterson tapped his pocket. 'But let's be clear. Let me explain the way they see it down at the station. I'll give you the list and we'll make sure there's no confusion. I'd hate for you to be confused.'

The detective took a few more steps towards the Eames chair. 'You work for Kasprowicz,' he said. 'You got all the Kass books for him. You lit the matches and wrote the notes. You're a helpful kind of guy. And you find Kasprowicz someone to kill his brother. Kasprowicz knew you'd find the right person. Because you worked for Ziggy Brandt, you knew every piece of shit in town.' The detective smiled.

Jack did not look up. He carefully shaped the end of his cigarette against the inside of the ashtray.

'So you hire Rory — he's nice and cheap, eat a bag of cockroaches for ten bucks. Everything is set. But then the fucker wants more money. Maybe he worked out he was being ripped off, somehow found out about Kasprowicz and guessed that whatever he was paying you was more than you were paying him. Or maybe he thought he could blackmail you. Maybe he thought he could squeeze something extra out of the deal. Is that why he stabbed you, Jack? 'Cause you said no?'

'You must be one of the five smartest people in the world.'

'I don't give a fuck why he stabbed you,' spat Peterson. 'He took the job. All systems go. Kasprowicz gets the fuck out of town. You're so dedicated to your work you get yourself invited to the apartment to see everything's been done right. And what do you find? Kass is dead and, hey shit, so is Rory! What a bonus! You're in the money now and no witnesses. How am I going so far?'

Jack hauled on his cigarette and then stubbed it out. The day had barely started and already it was up to his neck.

'That's a good story, Detective,' he said. 'Some twists and turns, some interesting characters. Motive's a little thin, though.'

'Not for Glendenning.'

Jack tried a grin. 'But the nice thing about writing stories is at least you can make yourself good-looking.'

Peterson burnt his eyes into Jack's. Half-a-dozen seconds ticked by slowly, as though a grandfather clock was in the room, marking time with long, ominous strokes.

The detective walked over and stood behind the Eames chair. He leaned in towards Jack's ear and spoke in a nasty whisper. 'What about the daughter? She good in the sack, Jackie boy? She part of the deal?'

Surprised, Jack turned his head a little towards Peterson.

'Why? You short on masturbation fantasies?'

There was a slight rush of air. An instant later the slap that caused it landed on Jack's right cheek. It snapped his head round to his left shoulder. His face lit up and glowed hot, as though a row of firecrackers had been set off inside his head.

Lois miaowed over by the bedroom doorway but thought twice about a rescue operation. Jack tried to get up out of the chair. The detective helped him up. A second later, he was sitting down again, doubled over and holding his guts.

'How do you like being fucked, Jack?' Peterson's face was red and sweaty: his eyes sparked like dynamite wicks. Detective Geoff Peterson loved his job. 'I hope you like it, Jack. 'Cause you're going to get good and fucked now.'

~*20*~

JACK HELD HIS HANDS OUT in front of him. Detective Geoff
Peterson put the cuffs on with a couple of swift movements.
He threw a coat over them, opened the front door, nodded
down the hallway. Jack walked through and Peterson
followed.

The detective's car was parked about twenty metres up
the road. Gusty wind whipped through the trees; drizzly
rain swirled and plunged in the air. There were not many
people about. Those that were walked by stiffly, heads down,
hunched under umbrellas, with mobiles and iPods glued
onto their ears. They paid no attention to Jack, stumbling
beside Peterson, the red welt across his cheek stinging in the
morning cold.

'That's the way,' said the detective. 'Nice and quiet.'

They reached the car, a white, unmarked Ford Falcon. Peterson opened the rear door and pulled Jack closer.

'In you get.'

Jack stepped back. 'I want to call a lawyer.'

'I'm going to count to one.'

'This is bullshit—'

'One.'

Jack braced but Peterson was too quick, unloading like a cannon. A hard fist followed by a lot of forearm, straight to the gut. As he doubled over the detective pushed him into the back seat and slammed the door. Jack lay on his side and groaned.

Peterson grinned at the *Neighbourhood Watch* sign riveted to the telegraph pole beside the car. He walked calmly around to the driver's side door, got in and drove off.

'You comfortable back there?'

'Motherfucker,' wheezed Jack. He squeezed his eyes shut and the darkness filled with wriggling shards of light.

'Good boy.'

Thrown like a sack of shit into the back of a car. Maybe it was just a bad dream. Or karma? *For every action there is an equal and opposite reaction.* The only mystery: when and where.

Jack remembered the day Ziggy Brandt leaned into his driver's side window, while his boys pushed some poor power-suited bastard into the back seat. Middle of the night. 'Take him out to Smithfield and dump him somewhere off the highway.' Ziggy pointed at the glovebox. 'There's something in there for you.' As Jack drove away, he looked. Even wrapped in an oily black cloth, he knew it was a gun.

His test. His moment. The initiation. Club membership for life.

In the back seat, the guy had pissed himself. He had a broken pinkie finger and a few bruises around the kidneys. He kept repeating his split-lip promise that he would never cross Ziggy's yellow-brick road again. Jack did not say a word to him: just glanced into the rear-view mirror of the big black Mercedes while the guy babbled. He drove straight to the emergency ward at the Royal Prince Alfred and left him in the car park. Then he went out to Ziggy's luxury city apartment, parked the car in the street, lit a cigarette and walked away. He was still waiting for the fallout. Ziggy Brandt was a very patient man.

Jack sat up, looked out the window. They were heading south. Not the way to the police station.

'I want to see Glendenning.'

'That's nice.'

'Where the fuck are you taking me?'

The detective smiled, said nothing.

Jack slipped down in the seat. His head felt like ten hangovers, his body like an old mattress thrown out into the street. He figured Peterson would probably drive him around for a while, cook him up a little. The Ziggy Brandts of this world were not the only ones who stuck it hard and mean to their fellow man.

They passed the airport, Brighton le Sands, drove towards Cronulla. The suburbs were quiet, damp, their leafy front yards deserted but for kids' bikes and garden hoses scribbled on concrete driveways. Australian flags were draped in the windows of a few houses, as though a parade had passed by.

They turned onto the highway, headed for Wollongong.

'What's down this way?'

The detective yawned. 'Gotta see a man about a dog.'

'You really think Glendenning's going to believe I had something to do with Kass's murder? He's not as stupid as you.'

'He already believes it, Jackie boy.'

'Just like that? No evidence necessary? I thought that was priests, not the police.'

'Who says there's no evidence?' Peterson grinned into the rear-view mirror.

Jack tried to adjust his wrists inside the tight handcuffs. Everything was starting to feel tight: his neck, shoulders, his lungs, his stomach. He looked through the window. Oncoming traffic drove by, people off to work. A nice job in a bank, his mother used to say. A cheap loan, buy a house, get married. Two or three kids. Live like a normal person.

They followed the highway for a while then turned off and took the coast road, climbing gradually, cutting through hill flanks thick with trees. Sharp morning sunlight pierced the clouds and dappled the car. Jack's ears popped. There were glimpses of the deep blue Pacific on their left. The coastline was all cliffs and jutting headlands and hemmed in beaches only fish and seagulls could get to. Further out the horizon was endless, blurred by mist and glare. Everything was big: Jack's life had never seemed so small.

Peterson wound his window down and cold air blustered in, raw and wet and clean. They passed Stanwell Park. A few more bends and then onto an unsealed road. It followed the coast for a while until it swung up into the trees covering a long hill. No cop stations here. No nearby neighbours either. Everything was perfectly still. The bush was damp with shadows, cold and silent. Jack listened to the car tyres splash through puddles and chew the coarse paste of wet dirt road. His uneasy feeling had a sudden growth spurt. He knew where they were going.

It was dark the last time Jack passed through, but he remembered the loaded calm around him: like a gun on the ground, just waiting for somebody to pick it up.

'So how's Ziggy?' The words caught in his throat as though they were written on wet pieces of cardboard.

Detective Geoff Peterson looked into the rear-view mirror. His face was hard and cold as tombstone granite. That Nazi face again. He returned his eyes to the road. 'Dying to see you, Jack.'

'And why's that?'

The detective shook his head.

'Come on,' said Jack. 'I'm not the corrupt cop. You tell me.'

'Don't think I can't deliver you with a broken jaw.' Peterson swung the car left, hard, just missing a huge rock by the edge of the road. Jack fell across the back seat, hit the door with his shoulder.

'Shouldn't be so touchy, Detective. The touchy ones never last.'

'I wouldn't worry about me if I were you.'

Jack flicked hair out of his eyes, stared at the back of the detective's head. He was trying to think, tune his thoughts, and got nothing but static.

'What does he want with me?'

Peterson laughed. He parked the car under a sagging pepper tree that somebody had planted for shade.

'Your balls is what he wants, Jackie boy. What else?'

The weatherboard cottage was at the top of a long climb of cracked concrete steps: a little hilltop hideaway where Ziggy Brandt liked to bring some of his girlfriends. Or sometimes his business associates—those who needed what Ziggy liked to call *convincing*. Jack had never been inside, never climbed the steps, was always made to wait down in the car. Looked like he was going to get his opportunity today.

The detective opened the car's back door and grabbed him by the arm.

'What's all this got to do with setting me up with Kasprowicz?'

'Move.' Peterson dragged him out of the car and up to the steps. Jack stumbled, his legs wobbly from sitting down. The fresh air was sharp in his nose.

'You're going to get into a lot of trouble, Detective,' he said, trying to believe it.

'Keep moving.'

They reached the top of thirty steps. Wet, ankle-high grass strapped their shoes as they walked over to another set of steps that led to some decking. Rusty nails creaked in the timber. Peterson held Jack by the arm and pulled open a torn screen door. He pushed a key into the front-door lock and swung it open. A musty smell: dead air and old carpet. The detective shut the door behind them. Jack had the feeling he had just been sealed in a box.

Peterson sat him down in a cane chair. He unlocked the handcuff on Jack's left hand and clamped it onto the armrest.

It was a fairly large L-shaped room with a low ceiling. There was a breakfast bar cordoning off a kitchen area down the shorter length of the L. Orange walls and a thin carpet of pale green. The light fittings were long tubes like cartoon torpedoes, with brass brackets. It reminded Jack of his childhood home. Not that he was comforted.

Detective Geoff Peterson walked over to a window that looked down the way they had come and peered through a crack in its dusty yellow curtain. Then he took his mobile phone out and stared at the screen. He pushed some buttons with his thumb. He brought it to his ear and listened and looked through the curtain again.

'I like anchovies,' said Jack. 'And get some garlic bread.'

The detective ignored him. 'It's me,' he said into the phone. 'I'm here.' He frowned as he listened. 'You think I've got all fucking day to hang around?' He flicked the curtain with a bony forefinger. 'Well don't piss about.' He snapped the mobile shut.

'You going to tell me what's going on?'

Peterson stared at Jack, said nothing. He flipped his phone open and dialled another number. He turned to peer through the curtain again. The hard look on his face softened. 'It's me ... Yeah, I'm down here ... Not till later ... I know, I know ... No, that's all fine ... Okay ... Don't be long, baby.'

The detective smiled and slipped the phone into his pocket. When he noticed Jack looking at him, his face turned into a fresh scowl.

'I bet she's a real looker,' said Jack. 'What's the cop discount these days?'

'You know what, Susko? I'm not going to hit you. I think

I'll shave your head instead.'

'How long you been working for Ziggy?'

'You don't believe me, do you?'

'Must be nice, the extra money. What am I worth?'

Peterson looked at him smugly. 'A dollar-fuck-all.' He glanced through the curtain again. 'This is just a small favour. A little token of thanks. Like a block of chocolate.' The detective turned back to Jack. He laughed. 'You look confused. It's your big gob, Jack. Spraying too much spit around. It was always going to get you into trouble.'

'What are you talking about?'

'Ask your friend Chester.'

'Sinclair? Come on, Geoff. You expect me to —'

'No joke, Jackie boy. He had plenty to say to me and Detective Sergeant Glendenning about you and all your wonderful adventures. Mr Brandt was very interested.'

Jack shook his head. *Jesus Christ.* Chester had asked Jack about Ziggy Brandt once, about his time driving for him. Jack had been vague: but all he had done was give Sinclair room to stretch his ridiculous imagination. Jack could see Chester talking himself into it with gusto, a whole load of fantastic bullshit, feeding it to the cops in buckets.

'Ziggy knows I'd never say a word,' said Jack, mustering a little confidence in his voice. 'And even if I were as stupid as you, he wouldn't go to all this trouble just to fuck me over.'

The detective walked round to the back of Jack's chair and ran a hand through his hair. He leaned in, close. His breath was sour: cigarettes and toothpaste and empty stomach. 'But this isn't just about you, baby.'

Jack turned, looked hard at Peterson. *Kasprowicz.* The old

man's name popped into his head, smoking like a piece of burnt toast. 'Where's Hammond Kasprowicz?'

Peterson pushed Jack's head away roughly. He walked back to the window. 'He's in Hong Kong, Jack, you know that. Doing a runner after doing his brother.'

'Bullshit.'

The sound of a car. Peterson put his eye to the crack in the curtains. He shook his head; a look of anger contorted his face. He sat down in the gold and red, floral-print couch opposite Jack. His right knee jerked up and down impatiently.

Footsteps over the timber steps and decking. The hinge-squeak of the screen and then the front door opening. Peterson looked up. Jack turned his head in the same direction. Ian Durst stood in the doorway. He glanced at Jack, then set his blue eyes on the detective. He put his hand on his hips.

'What the fuck are you doing here?' said Peterson.

Durst screwed up his face, tight as a cat's anus. He nodded his head as though agreeing with something he had just confirmed. 'Fucking Glendenning's onto us.'

~*21*~

Peterson stood up. 'What are you talking about?'

'He's fucking onto us!' repeated Durst. He was wearing a thick black coat over a stiff-collared white shirt and designer jeans. And, courtesy of Jack, a black eye and a bruised cheek, too, both turning yellow. 'He came around to my apartment asking questions.'

'About what?'

'You, for fuck's sake! He wanted to know if I knew you.'

Detective Geoff Peterson looked at Jack, then back at Durst. 'He's fishing.' But his tone lacked confidence. 'What did he say exactly?'

Durst walked into the room. He reached into his coat pocket and pulled out a pack of cigarettes. He lit up with a red disposable lighter and blew smoke with a long sigh.

'He said, *So you know Detective Peterson?* And I said no. Then he said, *But you've met him before,* and I said that I didn't think I had. I couldn't remember, maybe I had, you know. Then he nodded his head. Smug as all shit. The fucking cunt.'

Peterson stared at Durst and said: 'He doesn't know anything.'

'It's fucking Celia,' said Durst, sitting down heavily on the couch. 'She's sniffed something and gone to Glendenning.'

'You wouldn't be here if she had.'

'No, she has, I can sense it. She's not talking to me ... I can't even touch her ... She's looking at me with those crazy fucking eyes of hers ... I'm telling you, she knows.'

'Her old man's just been murdered, for Christ's sake! What do you think she's going to do? Have a fucking party?'

Durst's face brightened a touch. He looked at the detective for more reassurance but that was it for the day. His face went back to looking bleached. 'So why does she keep asking me why I went to the apartment to meet her, instead of the shop? I keep telling her it's because I fucked up the days, thought it was her day off, but she keeps asking ...'

'It's all in your head.'

'Bullshit.' Durst looked around nervously. 'Anyway, she's out in the car.'

'What? You fucking brought her here?' Peterson was not happy with the news flash.

'I don't want her going anywhere near Glendenning. If she's with me I know where the fuck she is.'

'Oh man, fuck me ...'

'Don't worry about it. She thinks I'm delivering a letter for a friend, to his grandmother.' He pulled an envelope from his back pocket. 'There's nothing in it.'

'Just like your fucking head.'

'Fuck off.'

'Amateurs. Always start cool and then lose it to paranoia.' Peterson put a finger to his forehead, leered at Durst like a school bully. 'She's got no idea about what's going on, just stick to the fucking story. Kass was dead when you walked in and you struggled with Champion and the gun went off and that's fucking it. Unless you talk in your sleep and told her that you hid in the bedroom and waited for Champion to do the deed and then shot him, she doesn't know a goddamn thing.'

'Better safe than sorry.'

The detective shook his head, looked at the floor. 'Glendenning's just checked your record that's all,' he said, his tone reaching for an ounce of conviction. 'Saw my name as the arresting officer when you got done in the toilets last year with the coke and that slut.' The detective turned and looked through the curtains again. 'Glendenning likes to be thorough.'

'How fucking thorough?' Durst flicked ash at the carpet.

'Don't worry about it. I can handle Glendenning,' said Peterson. Nobody in the room believed him.

'Well, you'd better. And you'd better make sure no connections pop up with that scumbag idiot Rory Champion, either. If anybody finds out—'

'I told you to relax.'

'You fucking relax!'

Jack adjusted himself in the chair. 'Not easy getting away with murder,' he said, as though to himself. 'Even with a cop on your side.'

'What was that?' Ian Durst stood up and walked over to the chair. He slapped Jack across the face. 'Every time you open your mouth, smart-arse, that's what you get.' He slapped Jack again, snapping his head the other way. 'That's credit. Want to say something else?'

'Sit down, for fuck's sake,' said Peterson.

Jack shook his head, rubbed his stinging jaw with his free hand. His brain ticked over, adrenaline-fuelled. He looked up at Durst and smiled. 'So you're the sucker with the gun.'

Ian Durst glared down at Jack.

'Glendenning went to see you because he didn't believe a word.' Jack stared coldly into Durst's eyes. Doubt flashed across them like a flock of startled pigeons. It was worth risking another punch. 'You sure you told your story the same way each time? Remember the order of things?'

'He's just fucking with you,' said Peterson.

Durst lifted his chin. 'When are they picking him up?'

'Later. George and Red are coming. Remember them, Susko?'

Jack looked at Peterson.

Durst grinned, his confidence returning. 'Yeah, that's right.'

George Papatheophanous and Red Sneddon. Two hundred and twenty-odd kilos between them. Each had the muscle-to-brain ratio of a brontosaurus. Ziggy's broom boys for cleaning up messes.

'They'll be by in a little while.'

Jack had heard better news. But he smiled. Rubbed his jaw some more. *Don't worry about the boys. Think.* Peterson and Durst had Glendenning on their minds.

'Hope you know what you're doing,' he said, looking at them both and massaging his cheek. 'George and Red hate complications. They're easily confused. Can't handle corners. Might be a good idea not to mention Detective Sergeant Glendenning going round to see Durst here. Remind me to keep my mouth shut.'

Peterson sat down on the couch, leaned his head back and hoisted a foot onto his knee. He stared at the ceiling and sighed. 'Sorry, Jack,' he said, amused. 'You're out of my hands. But good luck with everything.'

Jack looked at Durst. 'You do Kasprowicz as well as Kass? That wipe your slate clean with Ziggy?'

Durst's eyes widened a fraction: the whites were bruised and bloodshot.

'Sucker with the gun,' said Jack. 'Where'd you put him? One of Ziggy's construction sites? That place at the bottom end of George Street? Or the one on Castlereagh? Or did you go all the way out to Parramatta, use one of the new apartment developments he's got going out there?'

Peterson stopped staring at the ceiling, levelled a hard, dirty look at Jack. Durst glanced at the cigarette in his hand and dropped it to the carpet, extinguished it with his foot. Nobody said a word. The roof creaked.

'It's a good plan,' said Jack, as though he meant it. 'Kasprowicz kills his brother and does a runner. That's what you said, wasn't it, Detective? But instead of Hong Kong he's in ten metres of concrete foundations, under twenty-five floors of first-home buyers being smart with their money. Gone for a hundred years.'

'You read too many books, Susko.' Peterson stood up, slipped his hands into his pockets and assumed his natural arrogance. 'Made your brain soft.' He turned his back on Jack and walked over by the front window. Durst remained in front of the chair, arms stiff by his sides.

'What did Kasprowicz do to Ziggy?' said Jack. 'Shaft him on a deal? Or just beat him on the richest one hundred list?'

'You can ask Mr Brandt yourself, soon,' said Peterson.

'That was a handy little family feud, the two famous brothers hating each other. Was Kasprowicz really burning those books and sending them? Wonderful touch if he wasn't. Adds a nice bit of psychological complexity.'

Peterson smiled, flattered. 'It was perfect. The sick bastard had been collecting the books for years. Who wouldn't believe he'd put a match to them?'

'What about my shop?'

'Not quite pulled off.'

Jack spoke almost to himself. 'Kasprowicz didn't want to kill his brother.'

'Not in one go. Just wipe him off the face of the earth, slowly. Book by book. The prick.' Peterson screwed up his mouth in distaste, as though trying an oyster for the first time in his life.

'Just because Kass did his wife?'

'More than that, Jackie boy. More than that.' Whatever the more was, Peterson was not saying.

Jack sorted events in his head. 'Who came up with the idea of setting me up?' He nodded at Durst. 'Einstein over here? 'Cause it's all a bit on the vague side, don't you think?

After what, twenty, thirty years, why would Kasprowicz suddenly decide to take his brother out by hiring me to do the job? The details seem a little rushed. Not thought out.' Jack rubbed the side of his jaw. 'And I can get character witnesses, you know. I've been a model citizen lately.'

'It ain't about details.' Peterson's voice was level, business-like and cool. He knew what he was talking about. 'It's about confusion. Leaving a mess. Nobody likes cleaning up a mess.'

'Except lawyers.'

The detective managed a grin.

Jack smiled up at Durst. 'And you got all the dirty work. The most talented ex-gynaecologist in the universe with an IQ of three.'

The punch was not as hard as it could have been. Durst's fist slipped across Jack's cheek. He should have stepped into it: instead he had to reach and over-balanced slightly. Jack put his free arm across his face, expecting more. He watched Durst's nostrils flare as they juiced the stale air in the room for oxygen. It was another one of those times in Jack's life when he should have kept his mouth shut. But his mouth never listened.

'When you get done for all this,' said Jack, 'You can tell your daughter you're going to be the new butt boy in section D.'

Durst cocked his arm. Jack flinched, turned his head away. The punch did not come. He turned back to see Durst laughing, silently. Then he stopped laughing: his face snapped instantly into an angry, twisted mask. This time Durst stepped into the punch. Jack's bottom lip swelled up like a rubber dinghy.

'Enough of that shit.' Peterson walked over and pulled Durst away by the arm. 'You need to get out of here.'

'Just one more time.'

Jack swallowed a little blood. He ran his tongue over his teeth, checking for anything loose. They all appeared to be in place.

'Make you feel like a man, Durst?' he said. It hurt to talk. 'Take his handcuffs off.'

Peterson pushed Durst stiffly in the chest. 'Settle down, you fucking idiot.'

Jack said: 'You think a couple of tapes are going to keep Annabelle quiet after she finds out you killed her father?'

'What tapes?' Durst looked over at Peterson, frowning. He turned to Jack again and then back to Peterson. 'What tapes?'

The detective stretched thin lips across his small, pointy, tightly packed teeth. 'Annabelle isn't going to say a fucking thing.'

Durst ran a hand through his hair. Then he walked up close, bent down and put his face an inch from Jack's. 'Oh, I get it. Poor little boyfriend! Did the sexy lady tell him she loved him?'

Jack stared at Durst. Noticed the blue of his eyes. The ironed-out wrinkles. Smelt the expensive aftershave. 'Don't you know about the tapes?' said Jack.

Durst grinned. 'Sucker without a gun,' he whispered.

There was a noise in the kitchen, a rattling cutlery drawer. Peterson, Durst and Jack all looked up. Celia Mitten walked around the corner. Her hair was pinned back, her face grim and threatening even though her cheeks were flushed with morning cold. She wore a long, pale purple jumper over a long black skirt. The hem was wet in patches and smeared with mud. She was holding something behind her back.

'*You* killed my father!'

Durst looked alarmed. 'I thought I told you to wait in the car.'

'You bastard!'

She ran at him. She was surprisingly quick. Her hand came out from behind her back. There was a steak knife in her fist.

Durst leaned backwards, put his hands up as Celia lunged at him screaming. The knife stuck in his shoulder, in the soft flesh just below the collarbone. He groaned and then fell back onto Jack, still handcuffed in the chair. The white painted cane broke beneath them and they collapsed to the floor.

Celia managed to keep hold of the knife. It came out of Durst's shoulder, after she had twisted the steel in there for a bit. It had missed the padding of his thick black coat — blood was steadily staining the white shirt underneath. Celia writhed on top of him, trying to re-insert the serrated blade. Durst grabbed her throat.

'Get her off me! Get her off me!' His eyes were wide with shock.

'Bastard!' screamed Celia.

Jack rolled clear. The handcuff on his right wrist was still attached to the armrest; he dragged a large piece of smashed chair with him as he moved. His eyes were fixed on the doorway leading out of the living area. He commando-crawled towards it as fast as he could.

He was halfway across when the gun went off.

~22~

'FUCK, FUCK, FUCK,' repeated Durst through rapid, shallow breaths. His face was tight with pain. He pulled himself clear of Celia Mitten's body.

Peterson still had his gun pointed at the dead woman. He held it in one hand, his stance comfortable, his arm straight but not rigid. He did not blink: his eyes had seen it all before.

'Fuck! Get me something.' Durst rolled onto his side, away from Celia, holding his shoulder. 'I'm bleeding!'

Peterson shifted his eyes to Durst. The gun followed his line of sight, his arm swung around slowly, precisely. He pulled the trigger, twice. The bullets thumped into Ian Durst's body. One of them exited through his chest: thick, black heart blood spread quickly and smoothly and soaked his white shirt. His eyes were open, frozen. His last breath pushed a bubble of blood out over his lips: it grew for a moment and then popped, gone.

In a low voice the detective said: 'May as well be now.'

Jack looked up towards the doorway. *No chance.* By the time he stood up to run for it, he would be down on the floor again, heavier by at least two regulation police bullets.

Detective Geoff Peterson lowered his arm. 'Up you get, Jackie boy,' he said, as though nothing had happened. 'Over here.'

Jack pressed his forehead into the nylon-blend carpet. It was probably not even 10.00 a.m. yet.

'Don't make me shoot you.'

With some effort, Jack stood up. A piece of cane chair dangled from the handcuffs. 'Ziggy isn't going to like blood all over his carpet,' he said.

'That's his problem.'

Jack turned to the bodies: a strange quiet was already emanating from them. A cold, subterranean quiet. He wanted out of there. 'Glendenning isn't going to be happy either.'

Peterson pointed at the couch with his gun. 'Sit.'

Jack walked over to the couch.

'Arms out.'

With one hand, the detective snapped the loose handcuff over Jack's other wrist. It hit the knuckle of the wrist bone, sending a dull vibration of pain up his arm. His whole body was becoming rigid, cold as steel; the pain echoed through his limbs, bounced back and forth, collected in his head.

His jaw ached as though a clamp was attached to it, slowly tightening.

He glanced at Durst's lifeless body again. 'I thought you two were best friends.'

Peterson frowned. He held the gun up in front of him, as though he did not know how it got there. He turned it to one side, then the other, admiringly. He continued looking at it as he slowly stretched his arm out and pointed the gun at Jack. He angled his head, closed one eye and aimed. Then he shouted: 'Bang!'

Jack closed his eyes. He waited for his heart to slip back down his throat and then opened them again.

Peterson laughed. His eyes were wide. His forehead glistened with sweat. He had a sick grin on his face, like a clown who was starting to hate his job. Then in an instant it dropped away and his face tightened like a fist. He lowered the gun, held it against his leg. 'No more chances, Jackie boy.'

He turned and looked at Celia Mitten and Ian Durst, draining into the carpet behind him. 'Stupid bitch.'

'Lucky Ziggy's got more than one construction site,' said Jack. 'But you'll owe him. Big time.'

Peterson said nothing, slipped a hand into his pocket and pulled out his mobile phone. He flipped it open, dialled, waited. 'Yeah, it's me. You on your way? ... Ten minutes? Good ... That's right ... No longer a problem ... We'll just have to skip a couple of steps.' He hung up. He looked thoughtfully at Jack, his brain ticking over.

'How come I never saw you with Ziggy before?' asked Jack.

'Nobody's ever seen me with Ziggy.'

'You sure? I bet he's got a DVD somewhere.'

Peterson stared hard at Jack—no more grinning. 'Who says *I* don't?'

Now Jack gave a wry smile. 'Who says it'd help you?'

The detective thought about that. His face said that he did not like it.

'Got yourself a bit of a situation.'

'Not me, Jack. You.' He snapped open the mobile again and dialled. 'I want you to say hello to someone for me.'

'You calling the police?'

The detective ignored him. Somebody answered. 'It's Peterson. You can come down now ... Yes, pronto ... Hang on, there's somebody here wants to say hello ...'

The detective held the phone to Jack's ear.

'Yes?' asked the voice on the phone. It was an irritated voice. A woman's irritated voice.

'Hey Annabelle,' said Jack. 'It's me.' He felt surprisingly calm. Shock did that sometimes.

Silence from the other end.

'Don't worry, everyone's dead,' he added. It was as though his mouth was on automatic pilot. 'The money's all yours. You can keep the poetry books as well.'

There was a pause: Jack could hear her breathing. Was she about to say: *I wanted to tell you?*

She hung up. Peterson pocketed the phone, a thin smile on his face. He patted Jack on the shoulder. 'Love fucks you up, doesn't it, diddums?'

Jesus Christ. Jack had officially left the sane world. Everybody he knew was demented.

'So the whole time, you and her,' he said, his tone carrying a whiff of admiration. Then he sighed: it was involuntary. The new disappointment was getting heavier by the second.

But knots were quickly undoing in his mind, too. He could see clearer now, the course of events, the steady clicking into place of all that had happened. Mainly he could see that he was an A-class fucking idiot. The first painful step of self-realisation on the road to Nirvana.

The detective slipped his gun into the holster at the small of his back. He grabbed his elbow and eased it across his chest, stretching his gun arm like a discus thrower preparing for a heat.

'Nice plan,' said Jack. 'Ziggy fixes you up for delivering Kasprowicz, you get rid of a few relatives and the last bitch standing inherits the whole wad.' Jack remembered what Peterson had said when he shot Durst: *May as well be now.* How far back had their plan gone? 'All you got to do now is marry her,' he added.

Peterson smiled broadly.

'A lot of bodies round the place though, Detective. Must be worth it. What was Kasprowicz, ten million? Twenty million? Fifty? I suppose it doesn't matter after five.' Jack lifted his cuffed hands, scratched a cheek. 'Is Ziggy paying extra or was the deal just you kill Kasprowicz for him and he gets rid of the body? The quick set-up of good ol' Jack and then everybody catches up for a nice cold beer later? In Rio, maybe?'

The detective was still airing his teeth. 'Who said Kasprowicz was dead? That's going to be your job.'

Jack felt heat rise up his neck. 'Where is he?'

'Waiting. Somewhere. For you.'

There it was: the set-up. Nice and simple. *We'd like you*

to hold this gun and shoot. Jack knew nobody was going to give a crap about motive when all the i's were dotted by forensics. Not when they saw he had worked for Ziggy Brandt once upon a time. Looked like Jack was going to get his initiation after all.

'Sure Annabelle won't do a runner with the cash?' Jack wanted to change the subject.

'I got insurance.' Peterson's tone was casual, smug.

Jack watched the detective light a cigarette. Thought some more. Then he grinned, nodded, understood. 'The tapes,' he said. 'You've got the tapes of her in the sack.' It was not Durst at all.

Peterson blew smoke, returned the cigarette pack to his pocket.

'I'm not sure about these modern, open relationships,' said Jack. 'They never last.'

'You finished talking?'

'Have I missed anything?'

'You think I'd touch that fucking whore?' Peterson tapped ash to the floor. 'You ain't as smart as you think, Susko. You missed everything.'

Jack waited.

The detective laughed, dragged on his cigarette. 'I got the tapes all right, but she ain't fucking nobody.' He rolled his neck, a little to the left, a little to the right: a couple of bones clicked. 'What I got is her asking me to kill her old man. And her uncle. And her husband, too.' He smoked some more, shook his head. 'You'd think she would have remembered I'm a cop. We've got technology. It's in all the fucking TV shows.'

'Is that where you got your plan from, too?'

Peterson's face darkened. 'Just the bit about giving you the garrotte.'

Jack hoped Peterson did not see the shiver go down his spine. He nodded at the bodies of Celia and Durst. 'Maybe you could throw something over them.' Thoughts were banging around in his head, ringing like bells in a fire station.

There was the sound of a car below. As Peterson went over to the window to see, he said: 'She didn't do it just for the money.'

'Maybe it was for a bit of fun?' Jack's tone was bitter. 'The rich are easily bored.'

'It wouldn't be the first time that was true, trust me.' Peterson pushed the curtain aside with a finger. 'But not Annabelle. She hated Kasprowicz's guts.'

'That's nothing new. Why act on it now?'

'New information,' answered the cop blandly. 'Opportunity. What else do you need?'

'A dirty cop and a handcuffed sucker.'

Peterson wagged a threatening finger at Jack. 'Don't make me,' he said. He turned back to the window. 'Mainly it was she found out Kasprowicz wasn't her old man. Impotent fuck.'

Jack absorbed the information slowly. The detective glanced at him over on the couch.

'You ever meet that stupid bitch Sabine de Ruse?' he asked. 'She was married to Kasprowicz once. She found out he fired blanks. Squeezed money out of him ever since. Then after all these years she let it slip in front of Annabelle one night, pissed. All the botox must have got into her brain.'

Jack remembered something: Kass had had an affair with Annabelle's mother. He thought about that for a moment. Kass was Annabelle's real father. That's why Kasprowicz was putting together his little book collection. A revenge work-in-progress. And Jack had been his research assistant.

What had MacAllister said? *You don't know who's drinking and who's paying.* Jack was pretty sure he was going to be paying. He turned to Peterson, went to say something.

The detective was holding the mobile to his ear and held up his hand. 'It's me,' he said after a moment. 'Park your car further up and wait till I call you. Annabelle's on her way.'

'That the girlfriend?' asked Jack.

Peterson put the phone back in his pocket. 'Fiancée.' He went out of the room and came back with a copper-coloured bedspread. He threw it over the bodies of Celia and Durst.

'Almost there, Jack,' he said, looking down at the bodies. 'We're almost there.'

~*23*~

DETECTIVE GEOFF PETERSON did not appear outwardly nervous but he paced the room, smoked, looked through the window a couple of times. He went into the kitchen and made himself a cup of instant coffee, found a tin full of biscuits. He grabbed one and dunked it into his cup, holding the buttery goodness close to his chin. It occurred to Jack that Peterson had been a kid — once.

Think. Jack tried to wade through the swamp in his head. All he could focus on was how stupid he was. Was he any different from Durst? Suckered by a beautiful woman, completely out of his league. He was like a rabbit that had stumbled into an elephant shoot. And the whole slide into the mess had begun with a handful of goddamn poetry books.

'So whose big idea was all this in the first place?'

Peterson wiped crumbs from the corners of his mouth. 'What's the difference?' He sipped his coffee, then smiled as he swallowed, nodding his head. 'Oh, I get it. You're hoping Annabelle had nothing to do with it. She was forced to join in, had no choice, *blah blah blah*, mitigating circumstances. Sorry, Jackie boy. She's up to her tits in it, and she's standing on a box.' He put the coffee cup down on the kitchen bench and lit a cigarette. 'I told you already. Love fucks you up.'

Some time later, the sound of another car. 'Here we go,' said Peterson. He grinned and sat on the couch beside Jack. When they heard the knock on the door he called out: 'Come in.'

Annabelle strode into the room and took off her sunglasses. Her hair was tied back, accentuating the fine bones of her face, the harmony of her lips, nose and eyes. Hardly any make-up. She was wearing a black V-neck jumper, tight-fitting denim jeans and black suede trainers with white lightning flashes emblazoned on the sides.

Jack sat up a little. 'I've got the handcuffs ready,' he said. 'Just how you like it.'

Annabelle pushed the sunglasses into her red canvas shoulder bag and lifted her chin slightly. She looked down at Jack. She took in a slow breath through her nostrils and eased it out again—a sigh almost, but not quite. Her eyes dismissed him: pity mixed with contempt.

To Peterson, she said: 'Well?'

The detective nodded at the bedspread on the floor.

Annabelle turned, stared at it, expressionless but for the faintest contraction in the corners of her eyes.

'Both of them?'

'Take a look.'

'I'll be fine.' Annabelle reached into her bag and pulled out a white envelope that looked like it contained a small paving brick. She tossed it to Peterson. He glanced at the contents then slipped the envelope into his inside pocket.

'What about him?'

'Ziggy's boys should be here any minute.'

'Then I'll be off, Detective.'

Peterson stretched, reaching above his head with his long, monkey arms. 'No you won't,' he said through a long exhale. 'You're staying right here.'

'Excuse me?'

'I want you to meet my fiancée before you go.'

'What are you talking about?' Somebody walked into the room behind her.

'Me.'

Annabelle swung around.

'Hey Mum.'

Peterson had his gun out, pointed at Annabelle. Louisa walked across the room and sat down next to him on the arm of the couch. She took the gun from him, keeping it aimed at her mother. The detective beamed.

'I borrowed your jacket,' she said to Annabelle. 'I hope that's okay.'

Peterson reached out and rubbed her thigh. 'It's your jacket now, baby.'

Louisa leaned over and put her arm around his

shoulders. She kissed him on the side of the head, smiled at her mother.

Outside, all at once, rain began pouring down with a roar, pummelling the corrugated-iron roof.

Jack stared at Louisa's smooth, unblemished nineteen-year-old face. Then he had a look at Peterson's. Maybe somewhere deep down he had a beautiful soul.

'We've discussed it and we want a traditional church wedding,' said Louisa. 'Something small and intimate.'

'Who's going to walk you down the aisle?' asked Jack.

'Maybe you can,' replied Louisa without looking at him. 'Or maybe not.' The tone was beyond her years and all the more chilling for it.

'I think Mr Susko might be busy.' Peterson got up, walked over and stood beside Annabelle. The new son-in-law-to-be hugged her to him. She was still staring at her daughter.

'Don't look so shocked, Mother,' said Peterson. 'It's a lot of money you're getting. Turn the Pope against God.'

'And I love him, Mum.'

'And I love her, too, *Mum*.' Peterson was smiling like a spoilt kid born too close to Christmas, who always got two presents. Jack hated those kids.

'Does anybody have a cigarette?' asked Annabelle.

The detective reached into his pocket and pulled out a pack. He snapped the lighter. 'That's it, Mother,' he said in his oily voice. 'Just relax.'

Annabelle smoked. 'Did he get you a ring?'

Louisa smiled and held up the back of her left hand.

'It's not very big.' Annabelle dropped her cigarette to the floor, letting it burn. 'I warned you about cheap men.'

Peterson gave her a dirty look and stepped on the cigarette. His back was still to Louisa and Jack on the couch. He did not see his fiancée wink at Annabelle.

Jack did. His eyes widened and the muscles in his body contracted. He watched her stand up. For a moment he felt sorry for Peterson. Then the moment passed.

She fired three times. The detective arched his back and then his legs gave way. He fell. No last look at his love. No shocked eyes. No terrible realisation. Nothing.

~24~

ANNABELLE KASPROWICZ STRETCHED OUT her foot and pressed Peterson's arm.

'Think we should call an ambulance?' said Jack.

She ignored him, crouched down beside the body and reached into the jacket for the white envelope.

The detective's right trouser leg had come up a little. Jack could see the edge of a black leather holster strapped to his ankle.

'Let's go, baby,' said Annabelle. 'Quickly.'

'Can I get a ride?'

'I don't think so, Jack.'

'No? We could stop for coffee somewhere on the way, chat, have a laugh. Maybe some chocolate cake? My shout.'

'Always the funny man.'

'Better than psycho woman.'

Annabelle took the gun from Louisa. 'I don't want to kill you, Jack,' she said. 'That's for Ziggy to worry about. But maybe you don't need two nuts.' She pointed the gun at his crotch. Her lips pressed together into a hard line.

Jack had never seen this woman before. 'I thought you liked my nuts?'

'I like balls, Jack.'

'That's good. You'll get plenty in the women's penitentiary.'

Louisa walked over and peered through the curtained window. 'Shouldn't we tie him up or something?'

'We'll lock him in the bathroom, there's—'

'Mum! I think I just saw someone out there!'

'Get away from the window!'

There was the sound of a crash, of smashed glass and splitting timber.

Detective Sergeant Keith Glendenning ran in through the back door. 'Put the weapon on the ground! Now!'

Instead, Annabelle fired. Glendenning's shoulder snapped back, his body spinning around to follow it. Before hitting the ground his gun fired once: all the bullet did was put a small hole in a lot of air.

Jack dived to the floor, grabbed at Peterson's trouser leg. Then somebody started yelling from outside. More guns opened up, shattering the front windows of the house. He pulled the gun free of the holster.

There was blood on the sleeves of his suede coat. If only Peterson had grabbed the goddamn black denim jacket ...

He held the gun up, lying across the detective's body.

Annabelle saw him and fired. Jack fired too, squeezing the trigger three times. One of the bullets found Louisa over by the window.

'Louisa! Louisa!' Annabelle ran to her daughter.

Shit. Jack sprang to his feet and dived onto the linoleum of the kitchen floor. Glendenning was not there anymore. And the gun had slipped out of his cuffed hands, nowhere to be seen. *Fuck.*

He pressed himself up against the kitchen cupboards. He stuck his head out, looked across the room and saw Annabelle crouched over her daughter. After a moment she stood up, turned her head and locked her eyes onto his like a homing missile. Then she advanced on him, right arm stretched out before her, police-issue Glock in hand. The red flashes from the barrel did not correspond with the sound, like the discrepancy between lightning and thunder. A bullet hit the cupboard just above Jack's head. *Fuck.*

He dived through the back door. He landed in a lot of wetness. Fantastic. Now his two-hundred-dollar pants were ruined, too.

~ 25 ~

JACK RAN ACROSS THE STEEP BACKYARD, weaving between a clothesline, a brick barbecue and a small shed. He slipped into the trees edging the property. The rain was heavy, almost gelatinous, and already poured down the hill in rivulets. Jack splashed through, trying to keep his balance, but it was hard to run handcuffed. A bullet whizzed overhead.

The slope of the hill forced a diagonal path down: before he knew it, Jack was out of the trees and running across a bare hill-flank of sodden grass that dropped down quickly to the coastline and then vanished into a grey mist of rain blowing off the ocean. There was nowhere else to go. Not without a helicopter. Or a hang-glider.

Another gunshot. He heard the bullet smack into the soggy ground somewhere nearby. *Fuck*. He ran down the slope.

Three seconds later, over he went. He hit the ground, rolled like an unfurling carpet, then began to slide. The ground split open beneath him, he fell, but the ground came back again and he hit it hard with his hip, and slid some more on his side, like a human luge. His mouth was open but it did not help slow him down. Then something caught the handcuffs and nearly ripped his arms off.

Jack's wrists were torn with pain. He closed his eyes, tried to rein in his breathing. In a few moments he got it down to a steady *shit ... shit ... shit*. He could feel cold air blowing up from beneath his feet. He could hear waves crashing. He understood that he was dangling precariously somewhere. At least the rain had stopped.

It did not take Annabelle long to get there. She looked down at Jack hanging by his handcuffs and did not say a word. And there it was. The nobody-home eyes. Ziggy's seven veils look, just like he had warned Jack all that time ago.

'Hey, listen,' he called out. 'What do you say we get married? Right now? We could kidnap a priest and bring him back.'

Annabelle pointed the gun at him, fired a couple of times, missed because of the acute angle. She kept the gun pointed. When Glendenning called out she did not hear him, not even when he fired into the air. She took a step, down the slope leading into the ravine, tried to angle the gun. Fired again. Took another step: but this time found nothing beneath her foot. Her scream lifted all the birds in the trees. They flew across the sky like a torn black curtain.

Jack ducked his head, braced. Annabelle's body thudded into him, mostly catching his right shoulder. The handcuffs held. Her body flipped over his back. Jack stretched his head around and caught a glimpse of the silver lightning strike on the side of one of her shoes. Then nothing. Darkness. She had fallen off the end of the earth.

~*26*~

It was cold inside Susko Books. Jack's bandaged wrists ached. He kept his overcoat on while the heaters cranked up. Eventually they would stain a little of the damp air around them with thin electric warmth. With a bit of luck, in a couple of hours he might be able to loosen his scarf.

Wednesday. Glendenning had suggested Jack take the whole week off; but, bruised and tired as he was, hanging around home in fleecy clothing reading the paper had never been his style. The police had also offered him the services of a counsellor — to help him *process* what had happened. He told them he had Lois, and they nodded and said it was good that he had somebody he could talk to.

Jack sipped his long black. Lois had not been interested. Even the bit about Annabelle Kasprowicz being in with Ziggy Brandt from the beginning, about how they both wanted her father gone, had not sparked her interest. Or the bit about how Annabelle had set Jack up, at Ziggy's suggestion, by recommending him to her father, by letting it slip that she had heard of a good bookseller, then waiting for Hammond to call Jack and put their plan in motion. Lois yawned. He told her about the corrupt cop, the sad cousin, the lonely poet, the sex, the money, the body count, about how Ziggy had got away with everything because nobody could find Kasprowicz's body. *Whatever*, Lois had said. *Get over it*.

And to think that some people out there had to pay for good advice.

The phone rang. Jack put his coffee down on the counter and picked up the receiver.

A nasal voice said: 'You got any books by Edward Kass?'

Jack did not fall over but his heart gave a quick kick and a breath caught in his throat. Then he heard sniggering. He knew who it was. 'I'm going to burn your house down. Today.'

Chester Sinclair laughed harder. 'Feel free,' he said. 'I need the insurance.'

'But you'll be inside. With an apple in your mouth.'

'Now why would you want to do that? To your best friend Chester? The one who could make today your lucky day?'

'Are you moving interstate?'

'But the deal is, I want a cut.'

'Chainsaw or razor?'

'Sixty per cent.'

'Chainsaw.'

'Well, are you interested or what?'

'Yes. I would like to kill you with a chainsaw.'

'Come on, listen to me. You still got that copy of *From Russia with Love*?'

'Maybe.'

'What's it worth, five, ten grand?'

It was Jack's little investment. He was saving it for a rainy day. He remembered it had been raining since Saturday.

'You think I'm going to give you sixty per cent?'

'You haven't seen her yet.'

'Sinclair, you've actually done pretty well, you know. Working on two brain cells for most of your life.'

'Her mother's Japanese, her old man's Swiss. *Loaded*. He's a James Bond nut and it's his sixtieth in three weeks.'

'And she walked into your bookshop?'

'Why the hell not?'

'Fifty-cent paperbacks do not an antiquarian make.'

'The Swiss are canny with their money.'

'Canny?'

'Look, I told her I'd check with someone I knew who might be able to do her a good deal on a rare copy and then I'd call her. She's staying at the fucking Hilton.'

'Obviously watching every cent.'

'So? We in business?'

Jack took his scarf off. 'Not for sixty per cent.'

'Half.'

'Sinclair, if this isn't a big load of some kind of Swiss–Japanese bullshit, I'll pay you a finder's fee. Five per cent.'

'Fifteen.'

'Seven.'

'All right, a nice even ten.'

'Eight,' said Jack, pulling a cigarette pack from his pocket. 'Call me when you've worked out it's the number before nine.'

'Wait! Okay, okay. Done. I'll give you her number. Let me get the card.'

Jack lit a cigarette. His brain ticked over some figures. The Fleming book was worth anything between ten and fifteen grand. Maybe Sinclair was right: a lucky day after all.

'Here, you got a pen?' said Chester.

'Ready.'

'Her name's Leroux. Annabelle Leroux.'

Jack stopped writing. 'Are you trying to be a smart-arse, Sinclair?'

'What? That's her fucking name.'

'You sure?'

'Annabelle Leroux for Christ's sake! Come an' have a look at the card if you want.'

'Fine, fine.' Jack tapped the pad with the end of the blue pen. 'What's the number then?'

Chester gave him the number. 'Wait till you see her. A knockout. I love those Eurasian chicks.'

'You should have asked her out. Or were you wearing your tracksuit pants?'

'Eight per cent, Susko. And don't try and bullshit me about how much you get. I want to see the receipt.' He hung up the phone.

Jack walked over to the reference section and picked up the *OED*. Then he changed his mind. Today he would try the *Chambers* dictionary. *What kind of day? Good or bad?*

Bright or cloudy? He closed his eyes and opened a page. He ran his finger down the paper then stopped. He opened his eyes and read.

fain[1] /fn/ (*archaic* and *poetic*) *adj*: glad or joyful; eager (with *to*); content for lack of anything better; compelled; wont (*Spenser*). • *vt* (*Spenser*) to delight in; to desire. • *adv* gladly.

Jack Susko smiled. That the name Annabelle Leroux had slipped into his mind the moment before opening his eyes had nothing to do with it.